CONVINCING
THE
COUNTESS

BY ALINA K. FIELD

February 11, 2021
Previously Published in the *Misteltoe & Mayhem Regency Holiday Romance Anthology*, November. 10, 2020

Cover Design by Dar Albert

A penniless widowed countess with trade in her blood descends upon the country manor of her sons' negligent guardian, intent on confronting him and setting a course for her boys' futures. Instead, she finds his younger brother, a business-minded aristocrat with a penchant for widows and a distaste for emotional entanglements. A man who once witnessed her greatest humiliation. A man offering tempting distractions that threaten to derail all her plans.

Called home at Christmas to bring his older brother to heel and sort out the family finances, a baron's younger brother wishes nothing more than to finish the task and return to his railway project. But when he finds his mother entertaining a fetching widow he met many years earlier as the unfortunate bride of a ne'er-do-well earl, temptation steers him along a different track, one that may derail all his plans.

Can he convince the reluctant countess to set a course for her future that includes him?

Originally published in the
Misteltoe & Mayhem
Regency Holiday Romance Anthology

Dedication

For the many brave medical personnel, first responders, and law enforcement officers who have served with honor in our age of plague.
Thank you!

CHAPTER ONE

Richmond, 1811

"Gad, I've never seen the likes of it." Chester Halverton, Earl of Glanford, raised a shaky flask to his lips. "The gacking and puking go on forever. S'pose that's how it is when you breed on a woman who's not born a lady."

Good God, what an ass.

The Honorable George Lovelace shuffled a booted toe through the gravel and glanced at his chuckling brother, Fitz—Fitzhenry Lovelace, eldest son and heir to Baron Loughton.

Fitz leaned against the next column of the circular folly in the Townsends' garden, and stretched his legs along the stone bench he'd claimed for himself. "As the eldest of ten," he said, "I can assure you, genteel blood makes no difference."

The others—fashionable men of good birth, all Fitz's friends, all well into their cups—laughed and chided Glanford. They'd slipped away from the terrace and wide lawn through the arbor to this secluded folly to smoke their cheroots and drink something stouter than their hostess was serving.

"Surely your bride isn't ill all the time," someone said. "Did she not accompany you today?"

Glanford had arrived with an attractive young lady with wheaten-colored hair and wide gray eyes. Tall and shapely, she'd matched her escort in height and had greeted her hostess with a solemn air of either haughtiness or deep unhappiness.

George had suspected the latter. Now he was sure.

"She did." Glanford took another long drink. "Mooning about like death."

"Still, she's lined your pockets," someone said.

The ass brayed. "And easy it was picking hers. Lured her onto a balcony and one stumble later she was in my arms—with the right nosy gossip observing."

"Cleverly done," someone said, and there was more drunken laughter.

George pushed himself off the column. The party had been a dead bore, and this? There wasn't anything more tiresome than a bumptious fool's marriage woes.

"Let it be a lesson for the young ones like young Lovelace here," Glanford said.

Fitz glanced his way and shrugged.

Glanford belched. "Don't ever give up your ladybirds though, George."

He scoffed. "I do love tedious advice from my elders." At eighteen he had no plans to keep a mistress. He had better ways to invest the small income he'd received from his late godfather. "Yet out of my unfailingly deep respect for you ancient ones, I shall keep it in mind."

"Don't you want to know why?" someone exclaimed, ignoring his sarcasm. "Do tell us, Glanford."

He tried to catch his brother's eye, but Fitz's attention was fixed on the earl. Like George, Fitz was unmarried. However, Fitz did have a mistress tucked away in a lodging on Brook Street.

"No life there at all," Glanford said. "Like poking through a hole in the ticking. Heard wives are like that. Never knew it would be true."

In the general laughter that followed, Glanford turned a bleary eye George's way. "Find a bumbling girl with a purse, George, but keep your side piece, unless you like bedding the dead."

Everyone laughed, including Fitz.

He thought of the pain he'd seen in the lady's gray eyes.

"I've heard," George drawled, flicking at an invisible piece of lint, "a man has to make some effort. I've heard it takes a woman longer than two minutes to liven up. Unless, of course, one has engaged an actress."

Loud snickers followed, petering out as Glanford's face hardened. George forced a smile and held the ass's glare.

"Now, now," Fitz soothed. "What does my pup of a brother know about bed sport, eh?" He stood and slapped Glanford on the back. "George and I must be off."

Fitz nudged him along the path through the arbor, the men's voices and laughter following, Glanford booming out details of his mistress's skills.

"I've saved you from pistols at dawn," Fitz said.

Relieved to be leaving, George stopped, threw back his head, and laughed. "Only listen to him."

"He is an ass." Fitz was chuckling with him as they reached a turn in the path.

They both froze, their laughter dying. A lady stood rooted to the flagstones, a pale statue with wheaten hair, a far-away gaze, and hands twisted over a swelling waist. Glanford's bride.

"Said she learned the trick from a sword swallower." Glanford's words rumbled through the garden.

He heard Fitz's sharp breath over his own pounding heart.

The lady's gaze swiveled their way. Color flooded her cheeks and her lower lip trembled. He managed an awkward bow.

"Sophie." Fitz said, "are you well?"

She blinked, and a single tear rolled over her cheek, taking the color with it until she was as pale as the white gloves clasped at her waist.

Shame slithered through George. She looked ready to faint.

He took one step forward and she blinked, shuttering the hurt and freezing him in place with a stony gaze.

"Are you looking for Glanford?" Fitz asked, his tone gentle. "Shall I fetch him for you? The gentlemen are just down this path in the garden."

Her chin eased up in another long scrutiny, the steady throb in her porcelain neck pounding hard on his conscience.

"You are mistaken, Mr. Lovelace."

The words curled around him, the voice rich, deep, melodic.

"There are—and have been—no gentlemen in the garden today."

She turned, wobbled, straightened, and walked away.

Fitz moved to join her, but George instinctively pulled him back. "Give her a moment," he whispered. Their solicitousness might be seen as pity. Let her recover her dignity while she made her way back to the other guests.

They trailed at a distance. Instead of taking the path to the house, she continued on toward the drive. Assisted by their host's grooms, she entered a waiting carriage that immediately pulled away.

George beckoned the grooms, ordered his horse, and wished his brother farewell.

"Don't mind Glanford," Fitz said. "He means no harm."

"No harm? Your friend was abominable. Father would never be so disloyal to Mother." The lady's hurt and anger had been palpable.

Yet... he recalled her wealth came from manufacturing. It was said that she'd entered society with the goal of acquiring a title. "Do you suppose Glanford's lady knew the price of her rise?"

Fitz shrugged. "For the sake of the title, I hope this child is a boy. I doubt there will be any others."

He thought of her steely-eyed glare. "She's rather formidable."

"As is her father, and he won't be happy when he learns of this. That was Clark's carriage she climbed into. She'll be going home to Papa."

"Older brother or not, Fitz, if you ever treat a lady that way, you'll have my boot up your arse. Give my thanks to our hostess."

Fitz returned to the party, and George wandered toward the stable.

"I knew Clark," a groom said. "A fair man, he was."

"Aye. An' what sort of puttock would send his wife off on her own after such news?"

"What's happened?" George asked.

They exchanged grim glances. "Mr. Clark's died."

Hell. He raked a hand through his hair. "Does Lady Glanford know?"

"Aye. Her maid brought her the news."

Hell and damnation. They should have escorted her. He shouldn't have held Fitz back. She shouldn't be alone through this.

And yet...what could he have done for her?

"Hold my horse. I'll be back directly."

He found his brother on the terrace and pulled him aside. Fitz could deliver Lady Glanford's news to his fool of a friend.

CHAPTER TWO

Leicestershire, December 1822

Sophie Halverton, neé Clark, widowed Countess of Glanford, had sworn she was finished playing the dutiful waiting lady.

And yet, here she was, waiting for Lord Loughton's arrival, watching his mother, Lady Loughton, make the rounds of her drawing room where the family had gathered before the evening's planned dinner.

The waiting would end tonight, Lady Loughton had promised. Fitz—Lord Loughton—wasn't a bad sort, nor was his family. She'd bully him into a resolution, with his mother's help, if needed.

She sipped her sherry and pondered her achievements. She'd convinced Burford, the Glanford steward, he must visit his ailing aunt if he wished to be mentioned in the good woman's will. The moment he'd cleared Glanford land, she'd helped herself to the estate's ready cash and organized a paltry bit of Yuletide cheer for the tenants, to be carried out by the vicar and his wife. Then she'd bundled the boys and her maid, traveled to Loughton by stagecoach, and walked the short distance from the Royal Swan to Loughton Manor to meet with Lord Loughton in person.

It had had all been rather calculated and mercenary—either that or pitiful—and she hated the vulgarity of obsessing about filthy lucre. But she must confront her boys' guardian.

Unfortunately, Fitz was dodging her.

Fortunately, his mother had insisted she and her party move from their room at the Royal Swan to Loughton Manor, thus easing the considerable strain on her pocketbook.

For the millionth time, her gaze slid to the drawing room door and then to the knot of children grouped in the corner. Washed, combed, and carefully dressed, the three boys were twitchy with hunger and incipient mischief.

As one of the older children, her Artie, her little Earl of Glanford, was in attendance. Ben had remained in the nursery tonight.

Since their arrival here, Artie hadn't stopped smiling. Ben was just as delighted, though he'd prefer that the playmate his age—five—was a boy, not Fitz's young daughter Mary. They would both have a Christmas like the merry ones of her childhood. If she could but continue to swallow her pride and be grateful, she would have a happy Christmas as well, and perhaps, the means of visiting London at no expense but her time.

"You are here." Lady Loughton joined her on the ivory sofa and sent the children a fond smile. Petite and graceful in her lavender half-mourning, the lady's blue eyes glowed and strands of white sparkled in the fair locks peeking from under her turban. Her loving nature hadn't been cowed by the recent loss of her husband. Even Sophie felt wrapped up in the nurturing.

She set aside her glass. She must keep her purpose in mind. "When do you expect your son to arrive, ma'am?"

Lady Loughton beamed a smile and patted Sophie's hand. "Soon. We will wait a bit longer. Be patient with us, dear Sophie."

"Oh, ma'am, no, it's you who must be patient with me. I've imposed a full week on your warm hospitality."

"Imposed? Don't be silly. You're no trouble. Neither you nor your dear boys. There are always beds in the Loughton nursery, and with so many of my older children not joining us for Christmas, well, you see we have plenty of room. And of course, there's the matter of you taking charge of Miss Cartwright's launch. Such a godsend."

Charlotte Cartwright was another Loughton Manor guest, a wealthy tradesman's daughter, and schoolfriend to two of the Lovelace girls.

"Has Mr. Cartwright agreed to the scheme?"

"He will write any day now. And I've told him there must be a generous consideration for your troubles. New gowns at the very least. As for lodging, my second son and his wife will open their home to you and Charlotte."

"And my boys."

"Yes, of course. Unless—well, Arthur is of an age to begin his schooling. Or if you wish to delay, he and his brother might remain here. Fitz is their guardian, after all."

"Their father's death was a blow to them. I should like them to accompany me." Sophie straightened her spine and secretly crossed her fingers. "And I shall need more, er, consideration from Mr. Cartwright than just new gowns. Even with your son offering shelter, I shall have expenses."

The dowager patted her hand. "You leave it to me, my dear."

She managed a smile. The urge to trust Lady Loughton—daughter of an earl, widow of a baron, and warm-hearted mother of ten—warred with Sophie's well-earned distrust. The journey from wealthy mushroom to destitute countess had begun with one naive stumble into the arms of an earl. She had little faith left in any member of the aristocracy, not least herself. After all, she was more or less one of them now.

Earlier that afternoon...

As George Lovelace's traveling chaise pulled into the yard of the Royal Swan, a groom in Loughton livery popped out of the stables.

"Afternoon, Mr. Lovelace." Marty's gap-toothed smile never failed. "Cold enough for you?"

He shook his stiff legs and pulled the capes of his greatcoat tighter. "Damnable weather, Marty."

Marty laughed and fetched his trunk. "'Twill be snowin' here any day, my bones say. I'll just transfer your things to our cart and send this rig back. His Lordship ordered horses for the both of you. Just arrived back from Enderby a bit ago. Ain't even been home as yet. Don't know if he knows how the cold's come in. Been awaitin' you all afternoon snug by the fire in the taproom."

Marty plopped the trunk into the cart.

"Marty."

"Aye, sir?"

"He's been here all afternoon?" No wonder Mother had begged him to hie himself home and see to Fitz.

Marty cracked another smile, the glazed look confirming he'd been in the taproom as well. "Aye, Master George. And it being dark in an hour or so, I'd best get your things home." He tugged at his cap and turned away.

George shoved down his irritation. He could do with a warm fire and a brandy, but he'd have preferred them in his old room at home.

Inside, the taproom was teeming with men, all escaping the day's icy blast.

His brother sat in the corner, waistcoat unbuttoned and tawny hair straggling over a carelessly tied neck cloth. He looked bleary-eyed and bloated.

George scanned the mostly familiar faces and exchanged greetings, making his way over to the boisterous table near the great yawning fireplace.

"Brother." Fitz's big paw pounded his back.

The tavern maid arrived with a fresh glass, a full bottle, and a tankard of foaming ale.

"A toast." Fitz snatched the bottle and topped off drinks. "To my little brother George, the wizard who keeps Loughton afloat."

He'd forgotten to mention their other brothers, Rupert and Selwyn, who both helped manage the family's wealth.

George raised his own glass. "And here's to the new Lord Loughton."

Fitz's smile faltered. "And to Father."

After another round and George's report on the weather, the crowd thinned, departing to see to their livestock and their suppers.

"And how goes the railway scheme, brother?" Fitz asked.

The railway scheme. He signaled the tavern maid and lifted his tankard, stalling for time. The railway scheme, as Fitz called it, had been taking his full attention since father's autumn funeral. While he'd been off to Northumberland to look into steam locomotives, other members of the corporation were wrangling members of Parliament or meeting with landowners on the planned route.

His help was urgently needed with the last task.

"Coming along," he said. "A few challenges, here or there."

Fitz braced himself on his elbows and breathed brandy his way. "Georgie, I'm fuddled and foxed again."

George sipped his ale, waiting.

Of all the Lovelace men, Fitz was the most affable, the most garrulous, and the least business-minded. Father had moaned more than once to George, wishing sons two, three, or four had been his first-born.

Not that George envied Fitz. The title's obligations curbed a man's freedom. Once Fitz stopped grieving and accepted his fate, he'd do well. He could don his robes and attend Parliament, and leave managing most of the family business to his brothers.

Fitz studied his drink. "Mother wants me home. I'm glad you've come. The others won't be there. Not Rupert, nor Selwyn, nor their wives, nor our married sisters." He grimaced. "And still, Loughton Manor is swarming with females."

"As it always is." Besides their mother, Loughton Manor housed their younger sisters, Cassandra and Nancy, who were not yet out and George's young daughter, Mary.

"There are guests, George. Female ones."

Fitz's gaze glinted with humor.

"Your fiancée?"

Fitz frowned. "No. Miss Parker is at home in Hampshire." He swirled his brandy with a faraway look.

It had been a little over a year since Fitz lost his wife and newborn son. In September, he'd met Miss Parker at a house party, and become engaged within the week. Father's death had delayed the nuptials.

The sudden engagement to a girl Fitz had only just met, so soon after his wife's death, had seemed rash. "Having second thoughts?"

Fitz shrugged. "Rupert and Selwyn are abiding in London for the Yuletide, like sensible sods. Both Mrs. Lovelaces are increasing again. One of them is bound to have a boy." He topped off George's glass. "You know, George, you are the only one of us without a Mrs. Lovelace or an intended Mrs. Lovelace."

He laughed. At the moment, he didn't even have a mistress. He'd broken off with the last one a year ago when he'd headed to Scotland with his friend the new Duke of Kinmarty. "You're forgetting James and Edward."

"I won't count them until their voices change." His eyes glinted. "Mother is plotting."

George called for another tankard. He'd marry when he'd made his own fortune and not before. "May as well spit it out."

"There's an heiress afoot. Bound to be mistletoe and kissing boughs everywhere, knowing our sisters. You'll need capital for your railway, won't you?"

He swallowed a groan. "So much for the quiet family Christmas while we're still in mourning."

"Name's Charlotte Cartwright. Mother had planned to bring her out with the girls this season, before Father's death delayed their come-out. They were schoolfriends you see."

"A schoolfriend of Cassandra and Nancy."

"Yes, I know. Your tastes go to older widows. But...fifty thousand pounds?"

Fifty thousand pounds, for a lifetime chained to a girl like his younger sisters. "Tempting, but no."

Fitz laughed. "You didn't even ask if she is pretty."

"Is she?"

"Saw her at Easter. She's comely enough. Fair like our sisters. Not quite as much of a hoyden, I hear. Damnation, but I'd like to dispense with Almack's and all that bother and find our sisters a match in the country. Mother would appreciate having them nearby. I suppose their dowries are all in order?"

"Of course."

"Good." Fitz glanced toward the door and waved. "Come join us," he shouted. "George, this man has a high-stepper I want you to look at."

It was full dark when their mounts picked their way down the drive to Loughton Manor. While George dismounted, Marty caught Fitz before he toppled. The sight had both brothers laughing.

"In the suds, Marty," Fitz said. "It's his fault."

"Got to blame someone, milord," Marty said.

"If you see to these poor plodders," George said, "I'll be happy to take the blame."

"Always were a gentleman, Master George, even in short pants."

George laughed and hauled Fitz across the yard and through the kitchen door.

Their long-time cook squawked a greeting. "Your mother's been a-fretting. Waiting and waiting while the roast dries and the—"

"Our deepest apologies," George said. "We'll take a tray in the library." He spotted a footman. "Send word to my mother to start without us."

"We've just served the soup, sir."

"There you go," Fitz said. "We're not too late, and I'm famished. Haul me up there, Master George."

"I'll haul you to your bedchamber to change."

Another young footman popped in with an empty tray and Fitz grinned. "It's a family meal, isn't it, Jeffrey?"

"Aye, my lord. All but the very youngest at table."

"That will be for your sake Georgie. Everyone who can manage a fork present to greet you. Late or not, she'll want us there. Come along, brother."

As they climbed the stairs and made their way to the dining room, his heart lifted. He was anxious to see his younger brothers; they'd taken father's death the hardest.

He'd known that, and still he'd left immediately after the funeral, thinking that Fitz, the new head of the family, would tend to them until their return to school. Then Mother wrote saying she was keeping them at home for the Michaelmas term, and Fitz...

Fitz had let them down, and so had he.

***

Sophie spooned a mouthful of soup, her insides churning.

For the sake of her cook and the hungry boys, Lady Loughton had started dinner without Fitz.

Though she hadn't entirely given up. Not one, but two empty places remained, one at the head of the table, and one directly across from Sophie, and the footmen made no moves to clear away dishes.

"Who else is coming, Mother?" Twelve-year old James called from his place near the vacant seat at the head of the table.

"You shall see," Lady Loughton said.

"Is it Fitz's fiancée?" Cassandra asked.

Nancy leaned over her plate and peered down the table. "Why have you placed her between Charlotte and me, Mama, and not next to Fitz?"

Lady Loughton smiled.

"Mama," Cassandra said. "Tell us."

Sophie glanced at her hostess and cleared her throat. "The soup is delicious, my lady."

"Not too tepid?"

"Not at all," she lied. As in many great houses, the kitchens were a good distance away.

"Lady Glanford," Cassandra said, "you are purposely diverting our mother."

Just as Sophie opened her mouth to defend herself, the dining room door burst open.

"Here we are." Windblown and damp, Fitz filled the doorway and paused with a grin and a flourish. "And look who I've found. Your favorite brother."

A man appeared next to Fitz and Sophie's heart leapt into a gallop.

"I knew it would be you," Cassandra cried.

CHAPTER THREE

Sophie steadied her spoon and tried to quiet the bolt of instant, unbidden attraction, and the rollicking tumult inside her. Taller than Fitz, the brother's profile revealed a strong stubbled jaw, straight nose, and full lips. Dark hair brushed the edge of a white collar and crisply tied neckcloth; wide shoulders filled the dark superfine of a coat that tapered down to buff breeches covering the powerful legs of a man who must spend a great deal of time in the saddle.

Her gaze traveled back up and met blue eyes, and her breath left her. The same hard-planed cheeks, the same stubborn jaw, the same sardonic lips—but young Lovelace had grown into a shockingly handsome man.

It would have to be that brother.

She stiffened her spine as she'd done on that long-ago day in the Townsends' garden, fighting the sudden attraction, holding the piercing blue gaze. Oh, he was delicious, and challenging, and...interested. Heat flooded her insides and rose into her cheeks.

"George." The Lovelace boys swarmed him and pulled his attention away.

She took in a much-needed breath. She'd won this round.

As the tumult increased, she cast her gaze up the table. Artie squirmed in his seat, watching his friends. At the other end, Lady Loughton's lips twitched as if fighting a frown. Or a smile.

The woman had ten children, but this new arrival was special to her, and as Fitz said, a favorite of his younger brothers and sisters. He was equally windblown and ruddy-cheeked, and likely showing up for dinner in the same clothing he'd traveled in.

Her own father—another hard-edged man—might have done the same, arriving late from the mill after a business meeting. Her vision blurred again.

She shook herself and glanced around—anywhere but at him.

Across from her, Charlotte, her jaw dropped like a fish ready to take a hook, was craning her neck as this brother went to kiss Lady Loughton.

Loughton was betrothed. Was this brother unmarried?

He might be interested in Charlotte's fortune. Perhaps he'd be a good match, even without a title.

Sophie lifted her gaze again and found him studying her. He didn't remember her. Or he did and...his lips twitched into a lopsided grin.

Oh heavens. He was drunk—both men were. While Fitz shouted greetings to all and sundry and ploughed into his dinner, this Lovelace's gaze devoured her, promising things she'd never experienced.

And perhaps never would. The thought saddened her and cooled her racing heart. She'd once longed for romance, for passion, for true love, but ten years with Glanford...

At her age, it was best for a woman to shed that hope. Charlotte, on the other hand, was young and fresh.

If she was to bring the girl out...Charlotte would have a chance at a full season, a chance to meet someone worthy. Whether or not this Lovelace was worthy was an open question.

***

He knew her.

But from where? Foxed he might be, but desire flooded George, his gut and other parts recognizing this lady, who was no green girl from Cassandra and Nancy's school.

He fell into the loveliest gray eyes he'd seen in a long time—wide, and luminous, and equally interested—while his ale-addled brain searched for a name.

Hands tugged at him, and he tore his gaze away, greeting James and Edward.

When he straightened, the lady was staring intently at a boy about Edward's age, a boy with eyes the same shade as her own.

"Come kiss me, George."

Mother's voice pulled his attention from another split-second glimpse of a dark gown and a jeweled cross over a generous bosom.

"Mother." He kissed her cheek. "You look well. I'll change in a blink and return for the main course."

"You will not. You will join us this moment."

The footman ushered him to a seat across from the lady. His youngest sister, Nancy, sat to his left. The young lady to his right—fair-haired, blue-eyed, and rosy-cheeked—might have been Cassandra's twin, so much did she resemble her.

He dropped a kiss on Nancy's cheek, then inclined his head to the two strangers. "How do you do? I'm George Lovelace. One of you must be Cassandra's school friend visiting for the Yuletide, but which one?"

Next to him, the girl pressed her napkin over a giggle, her cheeks flooding with more color. The other lady went impossibly still and her gaze shuttered.

His breath caught. Face heating, he remembered.

"Do behave George. Lady Glanford, Miss Cartwright, you both know Fitz. This other handsome fellow is my usually punctual son, George."

Lady Glanford. He'd spent years remembering her hurt, her embarrassment. Her scold: There are no gentlemen in the garden today.

Lessons on gentlemanly behavior from an ironworker's daughter? Try as he might to shake off the shaming, he was grateful he hadn't. It had served him well in the wider world of trade.

A bowl of soup appeared and he picked up his spoon. Lady Glanford's lips moved in a stiffly polite greeting, stirring the devil in him.

Fitz and his fool of a friend, Glanford had been close once, but father had forced a stop to the loans and the gambling. What was she doing here? Had she changed much? Her innate dignity appeared intact. She was seldom in London, and their paths hadn't crossed there. He'd heard bits and pieces over the years, that the marriage had been preserved, somehow, and that she'd even given her feckless husband a spare.

Head tilted, she listened to Cassandra's babble whilst studying the new plate set before her, completely uninterested in both.

Her gaze lifted and met his, and held...and held...and...

Cassandra spoke, and the lady's eyes flashed irritation before turning away and releasing him for a view of the same porcelain neck with its pounding pulse.

Age had softened her. She'd been an attractive girl, but she'd grown into a beautiful woman. And with Glanford's death a year earlier, she was now a beautiful widow.

Was she the reason Fitz had delayed his wedding?

He shook off the thought. Fitz was more gentlemanly than Glanford, but when deep in his cups, he wasn't discreet. If he'd been dallying with Glanford's widow, he'd have mentioned it at the inn.

In his own liaisons, he'd taken the Glanfords' unwitting lessons to heart. He didn't pay actresses or ladybirds. His lovers were widows who relished their freedom, and he made sure he never left them unsatisfied.

This particular lady was free, and luminous, and...a challenge. And the house, Fitz had said, was bound to be filled with mistletoe...

Had Lady Glanford ever learned the pleasures of carnal love? And would Mother slay him if he pursued her?

His elbow brushed the flounce of a gown, and tension sparked in the guest next to him. The gray eyes across from him narrowed on the point where his sleeve touched Miss Cartwright's.

Nancy leaned close. "Why are you late, George? Did the wheel fall off your chariot? Did your horse pull you into a ditch? Were you beset by a highwayman?"

He elbowed her. "You minx. You're reading too many novels. It was nothing so entertaining. Merely snow. Bushels of it in Yorkshire. Dreadful weather, and the temperature is dropping. We'll have snow here soon as well."

"No one has introduced our friend." That was Edward, piping up in his little boy's voice.

A throat cleared across from him, and the lovely widow gestured toward Fitz's end of the table.

"Mr. Lovelace, meet my son, Arthur, Lord Glanford."

A new thrill rippled through him. He remembered her husky voice.

A dignified waif like his mother, the boy delivered a gentlemanly greeting, a contrast to the barbarian Lovelace boys.

"What of your railway?" James called. "Have you started laying the tracks?"

"Don't bore us with talk of railways," Cassandra said. "Tell us who you've been visiting. How is your friend, the duke?"

"He hasn't been visiting the duke," James said. "And if you bothered to learn anything besides embroidery, you'd know railways are not boring."

"My grandfather built a railway," Lord Glanford said.

Fitz looked up from his plate. "Did he indeed, Artie?"

A memory stirred: years earlier, Glanford had asked Fitz to serve as the boy's guardian in the event of his death. Father had urged him to decline, to cut ties with the earl. Yet here he was, on a familiar basis with the boy.

Lady Glanford's lips turned up in an encouraging smile that made his breath tighten again.

"It was in Shropshire," the boy said.

George cast about in his mind for a Glanford who'd built a railway.

"Ah," Fitz said. "You mean Clark."

Lady Glanford's father had been a partner in an ironworks. But in all George's preparation for this project, he'd not seen any mention of Clark building a railway.

"It was at the ironworks in Shropshire." Lady Glanford's voice filled the awkward silence. "At the time, my father was learning his trade, and he helped cast the iron for a small railway meant to run through the works."

Her son nodded. "It was an experiment to use iron for the rails instead of wood."

His mother's face filled with pride.

She'd been with child, that day in the garden, the day she'd learned of her father's death. Young Glanford had not heard this proud tale from the man himself. He'd heard it from his mother.

"And did it succeed, Arthur?" Mother asked.

"Not at first, but...Mama can tell it better."

Gray eyes glowing, Lady Glanford bestowed another fond smile on her son, before glancing at Cassandra who was pulling a face at her plate. The Lovelace girls were as barbarous as the boys.

"Glanford," George said. "I'll hear the story from you, but we'd best wait because the ladies will find it boring."

"Oh no, my mother will not be bored, and she knows far more about iron working than I do."

When he glanced across the table, Lady Glanford had focused an intense look on her son, delivering some unspoken maternal instruction.

"But of course," the boy said. "I will look forward to speaking with you another time, sir."

George's plate disappeared, and another replaced it, to the sound of his stomach growling loudly. His tablemates giggled, and he knew: Charlotte Cartwright wasn't a match for him.

"So, tell me, Lord Glanford, Miss Cartwright, have I missed any fun?"

His question set off a round of calls for sledding and games, gathering greenery and finding a Yule log, none of it requiring much input from him. He ate in as much peace as he could expect when he was home with this lot, and between mouthfuls, studied the lovely widow across from him.

After dinner, the nursemaid came for the three boys, and Fitz hurried off with them, saying he must visit his daughter. Before George could propose to wait for him in the library, Mother caught his arm.

"You'll join us for tea," she said. "I daresay you've had enough spirits today to last you a twelve-month." The twinkle in her eye softened the chastisement.

He laughed and went about turning up the Argand lamps and lighting more candles. As the room brightened, he saw beribboned pine boughs hung everywhere.

"Oh, sisters mine, I see your handiwork."

"Yes, and look up, brother," Cassandra called.

He groaned. A kissing bough hung from the ceiling in front of the fireplace. "I thought you weren't hosting the neighbors this year, Mother."

"What do you mean?"

"So much mistletoe, and no single men about to steal kisses from the young ladies."

Mother smiled. "We should have a jolly tune on the pianoforte. Lady Glanford, will you play for us again? We'll leave the girls to chatter among themselves for a bit."

"And let our food settle before Cassandra begins banging on keys."

Lady Glanford chuckled softly. "You may say the same about my playing in a moment, Mr. Lovelace."

The low mellow laugh and the saucy remark stirred him again. He took a seat on the sofa next to his mother and watched Lady Glanford move gracefully to the instrument, seat herself, and begin playing a piece from memory.

"She's lovely, isn't she?" Mother said in a low voice, studying her teacup. "I've convinced her to bring Charlotte out when the season starts, since we'll still be in mourning. There's no reason Charlotte should be held back with our girls."

"Did you invite Lady Glanford here for that purpose?"

"About that—we will talk. Your brother—"

"Fitz and Lady Glanford?" Anger sparked in him.

"George," Cassandra called from the other side of the room. "You must come and join us this moment."

"That forwardness of your sister, dear boy, is another reason to delay her come-out. Go." She glanced at Lady Glanford. "We will speak about the other matter later."

"Very well." He strolled over to the grouping of girls.

His sisters popped out of their chairs.

"Come and sit here, Charlotte." Cassandra patted the chair in which she'd been sitting.

"No thank you," Miss Cartwright said.

Cassandra patted again, making eyes at her friend.

"No, thank you, Cassandra." In spite of the room's chill, Miss Cartwright's pink forehead glowed.

"Then you sit here, George."

The sweet smile signaled danger, the kind a man regularly encountered with so many younger siblings. The chair itself appeared safe—the cushions were undisturbed, no frogs, pine cones, or knitting needles.

And she'd offered it first to her friend...

He glanced up. Cassandra had been sitting right under a kissing bough.

Nudging Nancy aside, he took her seat. Miss Cartwright let out a breath and bit back a smile.

"While you chat, Nancy and I will fetch more tea," Cassandra said and led Nancy away.

George laughed. "Those two nodcocks must have had you at odds with the schoolmistress at every turn."

She colored, smiled, and pressed her hand to her mouth.

"It's quite all right for you to laugh in our drawing room," he teased.

She nodded.

"Perhaps the ton will expect gravity, but at Loughton Manor, we suffer the reign of mischief and mayhem."

"And mistletoe as well, I suppose." She grinned. "It wasn't my idea."

Behind them, the music stopped.

"I don't doubt Cassandra and Nancy are responsible. But in any case, we can't let all this mistletoe go for naught. I shall persuade my mother into hosting the neighbors. Especially all the single young gentlemen."

A shadow appeared next to him, bringing a whisper of muslin and the scent of lavender. He jumped to his feet.

CHAPTER FOUR

Lady Glanford had joined them, her face so sedate it stirred the devil in him again.

"Miss Cartwright and I have just been discussing the Yuletide decorations," he said.

"Lady Glanford helped us with them," the girl said.

The lady bestowed a fond look on Miss Cartwright. "Only in the gathering of greens and tying of ribbons. The girls have done all the rest."

He slid a smile toward the younger lady, winked, and swept a hand at Cassandra's abandoned chair. "Won't you be seated, my lady?"

When she perched on the edge of the chair, Miss Cartwright pressed a hand down on another laugh.

"Come and play for us, Charlotte," Mother called.

"You might as well practice on us, Miss Cartwright." George turned in his seat. "Cassandra and Nancy, sing a duet for us, if you please. Miss Cartwright will accompany you."

Lady Glanford turned her chair to watch the performance, and he studied her profile, remembering. Mere days into her first season, Glanford had drummed up a scandal. Their marriage had spared the girl's reputation and Glanford's creditors. After, there'd not been one whiff of gossip about her, though her husband's antics had kept the scandal sheets aflame, at least in those early days of their marriage.

Glanford had been dead over a year, yet she still wore a somber gray, the gown simply-styled, the waist higher than current fashion. A thick bun at her neck tamed waves that glimmered in the candle light, dark blonde without a trace of white, and her only jewelry was a gold cross embedded with garnets. Her wealth—whatever was left of it— was not on display here at Loughton Manor.

"So, you are to be Miss Cartwright's chaperone?" he asked. "I doubt your services will be needed for the entire season."

"What do you mean?"

"She's a comely girl. A friend of my sisters, so she must be...lively. And I've been given to understand she's well-dowered."

Her gaze narrowed on him. "If I do this, I intend for her to take her time choosing."

He caught his breath. There'd been ferocity in that statement.

Miss Cartwright would be allowed a choice? How would Lady Glanford manage it? She wasn't often in London, and certainly didn't move in the highest circles.

"I intend for her to have every opportunity to meet worthy young men."

Ah. She didn't want the men of the highest circles. Men like the group in the Townsends' garden. Like her late husband, and Fitz.

And himself?

"Worthy?"

She nodded.

"And young?" He scoffed. "I'm not sure you'll find those two qualities combined in the gentlemen of the ton." He smiled. "Present company excluded."

Color rose in her cheeks and her lips moved up in an answering smile that didn't reach her lovely eyes. "Perhaps. In any case, I've a good eye for fortune hunters of any age."

"Her dowry will certainly draw interest." He recalled Fitz's belief that Mother was matchmaking, and this lady's sharp gaze at dinner when his arm brushed Miss Cartwright's. "Do you think I'm a danger to her?" He drawled the question like one of the rakes who frequented White's.

"I don't know you well enough to say. However, you are engaged in a business endeavor, and business endeavors always require capital. You are undoubtedly looking for more funds to invest."

"Or, the project may be fully vested."

The gray gaze pinned him, intelligent and challenging, stirring him. This lady was not just a beautiful widow. She might be a sharp businesswoman, if she was ever allowed to engage in trade.

"So, you and your partners foresee no problems? No cost overruns? No unexpected expenses?"

There were always unforeseen matters arising. The solving of them was part of the fun. Crossing swords with this lady was fun as well.

One slim finger tapped the arm of her chair. "Building a railway is not like commissioning a shipload of goods, where a gentleman, on the expectation of great profits, might sink a fixed amount, perhaps all of his wealth and then some, and learn it has been lost to the Barbary pirates with every hand, every bottle, and every crate." The tapping accelerated. The steady gaze darkened. "In such a case, one loses in one fell swoop. For example, as one might have, if one invested in the Matilda Rose."

The Matilda Rose? Why bring that up? The ship had been lost years ago. Plenty of fellows had lost money, but not him. On his father's advice, he'd withdrawn from the risky investment, and so had Fitz.

He shoved down a nagging unease, gave into annoyance, and forced a laugh. "My dear Lady Glanford. It's rare to meet a woman so well versed in business." He leaned forward in his chair and lowered his voice. "Perhaps I'll be a danger to you. Do you know, you are seated under the mistletoe?"

Her finger stilled. She stood and extended her hand.

No rings, no bracelets, no other adornments. He bent over white fingers and brought them firmly against his lips.

Her shiver shook him down to the soles of his boots.

"There." Under the steady gray gaze, the pulse in her neck ticked. "I shall be more careful in the future, Mr. Lovelace."

"I'm going up," Mother announced. "George, you'll escort me. Girls, don't keep Lady Glanford up late."

At the door, he cast a glance back and caught the lady in question watching him. She dropped her gaze and turned away.

So, she was not unaffected either.

Mother sailed along on his arm with nary a limp or a creak of her bones, yet she seemed thinner, more fragile since his father's funeral.

"Retiring early, aren't you?" he asked.

"Not so early. You'll remember that dinner was late."

Mother could, and often did, stay up until dawn for parties and balls. Father had shared her love of society. It was no wonder she wanted her children at home for this first Christmas without him.

Though, he knew, that wasn't the main reason she'd called him home.

As they ascended the steps, he plunged in. "What the devil is wrong with Fitz, Mother?"

"You're just like your father," she said. "Right to the point. I do miss him so."

"I know. While we're getting to the point, tell me also why Lady Glanford is here."

She paused as they reached the landing. "What think you of Charlotte, George? She's very eligible."

"She's a lovely young girl, and I don't wish to marry her."

"Well, I tried." Smiling, she turned and presented her cheek to him, pointing up at the ceiling, where a kissing bough hung. "I may as well take advantage."

George laughed, dropping a kiss on her cheek. "You're still lovely as ever, Mama."

"And not looking for a spouse either, so don't even mention the notion."

"No one could replace Father."

She squeezed his hand and led him along to her private sitting room, dismissing her maid, and seating him next to her on the settee.

"I wish your father were here," she said. "And Grumby as well."

Grumby was their longtime steward. "He's gone?"

"He's never quite recovered from the fever that took your father's life. I've given him leave to spend time with his sister." She sighed. "I'm afraid neither he nor Fitz are seeing to the business of Loughton. Fitz comes home for a few days and is off again. His friends are a wild set. I thought, after Glanford died—"

"Fitz was still entangled with Glanford?"

"I fear so, though he kept it from your father."

"And Lady Glanford's visit?"

"The poor dear traveled by stagecoach, left the boys and her maid at the Swan, and turned up on my doorstep. She was determined to wait at the Swan until Fitz returned. Of course, I insisted she move in here with us."

"Of course. But...she came to see Fitz?"

"The boys are delightful. I wouldn't mind keeping them, if Fitz wishes and she agrees. Arthur might go off to school with James and Edward. They would enjoy that." She squeezed his hand. "Sophie has been good with all the children, and has helped a great deal with the Yuletide preparations." She studied the flames licking the grate. "I sense that she greatly needs help, and Fitz is her boys' guardian."

"She might have written Fitz with her concerns."

"She said she has, and I believe that's true. I've seen letters posted from Lancashire."

If Fitz was ignoring his own family responsibilities, it was certain he wasn't concerning himself with Glanford's.

"She revealed nothing more?"

"No, and I didn't wish to pry. She has a shield about her, but I sense her distress. I want you to get to the bottom of it, George. Talk to Fitz."

He stood. "I'll do so, first thing."

"Tomorrow is soon enough. You must be exhausted after your long journey."

She followed him to the door and turned her cheek up again for a kiss. "I'm so glad you're here. Not just for Fitz's sake, but for the others as well. The boys have been tormenting the life out of the girls."

He patted her hand and wished her a goodnight.

*****

It was well on to midnight when Sophie shepherded the girls up to their bedchambers and climbed the stairs to the nursery suite. She kissed Ben, and then tucked the covers around Artie, not at all sure he and his chamber mates, James and Edward, were truly asleep. Even if they stayed up half the night whispering when she left, she was grateful they weren't alone in the freezing cold manor house entailed to the Earl of Glanford.

She wished the nursery maid a good night and slipped down the stairs to the guest suite she shared with her maid.

Willa jumped from the chair by the roaring fire, where she'd been dozing.

"It's toasty in here," Sophie said, casting aside her shawl.

"And my old joints are grateful, dear one. I'm right glad we're here. Come through and let's get you undressed."

Sophie followed the maid into the small room that contained a cot and a collection of loaned garments.

Willa addressed the gown's laces. "I hear his lordship is here," she said. "And?"

"And oh, for the days when I was just plain Sophie Clark."

"You've never been plain. You mean rich Sophie Clark."

"And single Sophie Clark." A widowed viscount had expressed interest in her, other younger men of the ton, as well. They were all, of course, after her dowry. Even in the first bloom of youth, she hadn't been a diamond of the first water.

Glanford had called her a diamond in the rough. Among other things.

What a fool she'd been. Her sponsor had warned her against fortune hunters. But a walk on a balcony at a crowded ball with Glanford and a new lady acquaintance had seemed harmless.

So delighted that his daughter had "captured" an earl, Papa had tossed aside his shrewdness and common sense. His daughter would be a countess. The rushed wedding was lavish, her gown exquisite, her wedding pearls the best Papa could buy.

The pearls were gone, as was all of the jewelry known to Glanford and his creditors; all but her grandmother's garnet cross.

Willa helped settle a nightgown over her head and gathered her discarded clothing.

She seated herself at the dressing table and began taking down her hair while Willa chattered.

"I heard from the housekeeper at Glanford. Most of the girls have found places."

Her stomach churned. She, a commoner, a nobody, had all but closed up the ancestral home of the Earl of Glanford. Even before Glanford's death, the steward had begun the letting go of staff and selling off all but the draft horses and the mount that carried Glanford on his ill-fated ride for the foxes.

"Do not you worry, Sophie. You fed half the hungry mouths of Lancashire and saw the sick were tended. All know what you endured."

She squeezed her eyes and took in a breath. "I have no need for pity."

Willa took the brush from her hand. "Is Loughton ignoring you?"

"He's only just arrived home."

"Best he sober up I s'pose. Spent all afternoon in the taproom, I hear. That's a guilty conscience. And the brother just as sopped." Willa harrumphed. "And now off we go to London, saddled with Miss Cartwright."

Sophie bit back the urge to scold and reached for her face cream. Frown lines were forming, just as Willa had warned since she was Ben's age. "Chaperoning Miss Cartwright is a great opportunity." Given her lowly roots, her late husband's character, and her insignificant social ties, she'd been surprised by the request. "We'll have shelter with Mr. and Mrs. Lovelace, food on the table, and coal in the grate. And I know you appreciate a warm fire."

And in London, she could find time to conduct some private business of her own.

She reached for her dressing gown. "I'll read for a while. Take yourself off to bed, Willa."

When the door to the dressing room closed, she paced to the bedside table, picked up the novel she'd borrowed from the Loughton library, and set it back down.

Christmas was three days away and as delighted as she was to be able to celebrate a proper Yuletide, Willa's wages were due. Paying her loyal maid would bide for now, but what was she to do about gifts for the children, Boxing Day presents, vails for the Loughton staff?

Her stomach churned again. Dinner had been a travesty of picking at food, barely tasting it. Fitz had been too bosky for a serious conversation, and his brother...

He was handsome, and he knew it. And he raised feelings in her. Little use was her set-down over the Matilda Rose—Lovelace had retaliated with his lips. That kiss on the hand had been disturbingly...intimate.

With a tremendous rumble, her stomach informed her she shouldn't have picked at the good dinner.

The cook here was a generous sort who'd joked with the boys about their nighttime raids. Perhaps she could find a biscuit and warm some milk.

She slipped into her shoes, and made her way down the corridor to the stairs.

CHAPTER FIVE

At the next landing, she spotted the door to the library ajar and heard a male voice.

If Fitz was still awake, perhaps she might approach him now. She edged closer.

"I'm as surprised as you are to find Sophie here."

That was Fitz. Who was with him?

"Sophie, is it?"

Lovelace was here, and his tone held contempt.

"It's not like that, George."

"Hmm. She's grown even comelier with age."

She pressed a hand to her hammering heart. She'd felt his attraction, both when he'd ogled her during dinner, and later, with that kiss. Now, all she heard was disdain.

Were all men false when they were out of earshot?

"Are you interested, George? I should protest, perhaps challenge you. I'm the nearest thing to a protector...Not that sort of protector. I'm sole guardian of her boys."

"Sole?"

"The other died. Glanford, with his usual attention to his responsibilities, never amended his arrangements before he cocked up his heels."

"I see."

She drew nearer, holding her breath for whatever else Fitz might reveal.

"Mother told me she simply appeared a week ago," Lovelace said.

Heat rose in her cheeks. While she'd been overseeing the girls, George Lovelace and Lady Loughton had been gossiping about her.

"A countess traveling alone with her boys— your wards—by public coach."

Still a vulgar upstart, that Sophie Clark. She held her breath through another long pause and finally Fitz spoke.

"You are interested. She hasn't a farthing, and you need money for your railway scheme. The heiress is a better bet."

"Miss Cartwright is a child."

"A child with a sizeable dowry. Sophie's is gone. She'd bring nothing to a marriage but two extra mouths, and for you to keep her might subject my wards to scandal. And deplete your purse, and I know how prudent you are about money. Though I suppose, whatever might happen here between the two of you under the mistletoe..." Fitz laughed. "No, there are too many small ears and eyes about, besides Mother's. Don't even try it."

Angry tears sprang to her eyes, and she beat them back. She was a widow, and to the men of the ton, widows were fair game. Fitz and his brother were still thoughtless and just as calculating as every other nobleman.

Head pounding, she hurried past the door. Her conversation with Fitz would keep.

She found her way to the narrow servants' stairs, where the upstart Sophie Clark belonged.

Moments earlier...

"Still awake?"

Fitz looked up and grunted, holding out an empty glass. "Pour me one, will you, George?"

"As if we haven't had enough for one day." He took the glass.

Unable to sleep, George had rummaged through an old wardrobe for a dressing gown and then headed down to the library. As he'd expected, he found Fitz by the fire, boots propped on the fender, still fully dressed.

Good, because he had questions.

He filled two glasses and took the opposite wingchair.

"Here's to Father," Fitz said.

George raised his tumbler and drank, deciding how to begin. Fitz was his older brother, and the head of the family now. He owed him some deference. On the other hand, they were brothers and Fitz was conducting himself like an ass. Plus, he needed to finish here and attend to his own business.

So, the direct approach. "What the devil is going on with you, Fitz? Mother wrote me that you've been in a funk."

Fitz's feet plopped to the floor.

"Don't leave," George said. "I've hardly had a chance to speak to you."

"We had all afternoon at the Swan."

"Which we spent mostly discussing horses. Tell me, what is Glanford's widow doing here?"

Fitz's eyes focused. "You don't wish to ask about the heiress?"

He was deflecting. The late Earl of Glanford was a sore subject to Fitz.

"I'm as surprised as you are to find Sophie here," Fitz said.

"Sophie, is it?"

Fitz waved a hand. "It's not like that."

"Hmm. She's grown comelier with age."

Fitz eyed him over his glass and smiled slyly. "Are you interested, George? I should protest, perhaps challenge you. I'm the nearest thing to a protector—" He held up a hand. "Not that sort of protector. I'm sole guardian of her two boys."

"Sole?"

"The other died. Glanford, with his usual attention to his responsibilities, never amended his arrangements before he cocked up his heels."

"I see."

Fitz harrumphed and fell deep into frowning.

"Mother said she simply appeared a week ago." George swirled the brandy, watching his brother out of the corner of his eye. "A countess traveling alone with her boys—your wards—by public coach."

Of course, Mother wouldn't—couldn't, by all that was honorable—turn her or her boys away.

Fitz lounged back, his gaze hooded. "You are interested. She hasn't a farthing, and you need money for your railway scheme. The heiress is a better bet."

"Miss Cartwright is a child." He stood and fetched a bottle from the sideboard.

"A child with a sizeable dowry. Sophie's is gone. She'd bring nothing to a marriage but two extra mouths, and for you to keep her might subject my wards to scandal. And deplete your purse, and I know how prudent you are about money. Though I suppose, whatever might happen here between the two of you under the mistletoe..." Fitz laughed and glanced toward the door. "No, there are too many small ears and eyes about, besides Mother's. Don't even try it."

He beamed him the flim-flamming smile he used to charm his way out of trouble.

A shadow flashed in the corridor, like a ghost scurrying by. Or, since Loughton Manor wasn't haunted, a Lovelace chit. At this hour, the servants were abed. One of his sisters was roaming the Manor.

"I shall be watching, as well," Fitz said.

"Good." He refilled Fitz's glass and set the bottle on the table beside him. "We'll talk more tomorrow. I've heard from Selwyn about the tax levies. Perhaps we can talk during a morning ride?"

Fitz waved a hand and George left him staring into the fire.

What the devil was Fitz running away from? Tomorrow, he'd get his brother out for a brisk ride, and then sit him down to go over the books.

He stepped into the corridor, listening. The figure had moved toward the servants' stairs. He headed that way.

CHAPTER SIX

When he reached the bottom of the stairs, George heard voices and paused.

"It's the artillery for me."

That was his brother James.

"And I'm going to build things."

Edward was here also.

"So am I."

"You can't, Artie," Edward cried. "You're a lord."

"So what? I'm going to open a foundry and run it. Mother says we have ore on our land. Isn't that right, Mama?'

His heart quickened. The figure gliding past the library hadn't been one of his sisters. Lady Glanford was here.

How much had she heard of his conversation with Fitz? He was destined for more shaming.

"Yes, I believe so," she said.

"But how can you know?" James asked.

"Grandfather taught her," Artie said. "My mother wanted to run Grandfather's business. It was her dream."

"Ladies don't run businesses," James said.

"Why not, James?" she asked. "Even ladies must be allowed to dream, don't you think? I intend to help Artie with his foundry in any way I can."

A long pause ensued while his brothers considered the startling notion of a lady dreaming about running a business. The cheerful note in her voice had surprised even him—Glanford apparently hadn't crushed her spirit. She'd not entirely given up the dream, and she was grooming her son to be more like her father. Or herself.

"May we have another biscuit?" Artie asked.

"Truly, my dear lady, Cook will not mind." His voice breaking with budding adolescence, James was trying some gentlemanly charm.

George and his older brothers had sneaked out of the nursery on many nights, exploring the Manor, and sometimes the grounds, unsupervised. They often ended with a raid on Cook's pantry.

"Pleathe, Mama." That was the lisp of a very young child.

"Oh alright. Just one more each."

George crept stealthily into the kitchen.

Four boys huddled on benches at the worktable. The lady was nowhere in sight.

"What's going on here?" he roared.

They shrieked, an arm shot out, and a mug rolled away, flooding the wooden table with milk. When he walked into the candlelight, the cries turned into laughter, and his two brothers attacked him.

Lady Glanford raced from the pantry. The smallest boy flung himself into her free arm and she juggled the boy and the plate like a waiter at White's steadying some drunken sod.

"Mr. Lovelace."

Candlelight glowed in her eyes and shimmered in a bronzed cascade of hair that took his breath away.

He tore his gaze away and swatted at Edward. "I beg your pardon, my lady. I couldn't resist frightening these two nodcocks."

Artie mopped at a pool of milk with the sleeve of his nightshirt.

"Not your sleeve, Artie." Lady Glanford set down the plate, and tossed a tea towel, still clutching the smallest boy.

"I didn't think about frightening your boys," George said. "I beg your pardon,"

"As you should." She settled the boy back on the bench.

"George always scares us." James elbowed the child. "Don't be afraid, Ben. And don't worry. We'll repay him when he least expects it."

"You'll do no such thing, Ben and Arthur. We are guests here." Lady Glanford slid the plate into the center. Four biscuits sat squarely in the middle, one atop the other.

He leaned against the sideboard, watching. A too-short dressing gown revealed trim ankles and shapely limbs. She must have borrowed nightclothes from his shorter sisters. In her dishabille, she looked closer to twenty than...how old was she? Surely past thirty.

The little boy glanced back at him. Like his brother, he had Sophie's eyes.

"So, you are Ben. I'm pleased to meet you."

"Tell her George," Edward said. "Tell her Cook keeps the biscuits in the pantry for us. I want another. Lady Glanford doesn't believe us."

She raised her eyebrows at him, making him laugh.

"It's true, my lady. Cook spoils these Lovelace brats. I'll fetch them."

"No, I will. But let Cook's wrath be on your head, Mr. Lovelace. The nursemaid's as well, when they all toss and turn with the stomach ache."

He bowed. She scoffed, picked up a candle, and entered the storeroom.

"We're glad you're here," James said. "We've been going mad with boredom."

"Mother said you've been tormenting the girls."

James shrugged. "I wish she had let us go back to school. And it's them tormenting us. You can't imagine the fits Cassandra threw when Mother told her she was delaying her come-out. I wanted to thrash her."

George swallowed a laugh. "A gentleman doesn't strike—"

"Yes, I know. But after Charlotte arrived and Lady Glanford took us out to gather greenery, the girls ran about plotting and hanging kissing boughs everywhere."

Edward scrunched his face into a frown over his milk moustache. "Cassandra says it's time for you to marry, and that you're going to marry Charlotte."

He choked, grabbed Edward's mug and took a drink, weighing the best time to throttle his sister.

"But Charlotte is too silly for you," Edward continued. "Cassandra was fretting that you might like Lady Glanford better. I do. I think you should marry her."

"Exthept, we don't have a feather to fly with." Ben broke his silence cheerfully around a mouthful of biscuit.

Artie shot his brother a look. "Don't speak when you're chewing."

"If George marries Lady Glanford, we'll be brothers," Edward said, warming to the argument.

James thumped Edward's head. "You numbskull. George is our brother. He'd be their stepfather. Which would make us their uncles."

"Don't hit me," Edward shouted, and they were off on a noisy dispute.

He snatched up both his brothers and squeezed between them. "Do you want to argue, or do you want to hear about my railway?"

***

While the conversation continued in the kitchen, Sophie paused set her candle on a box in the larder and pressed a hand to her chest. Thank God the boys were here. Mr. Lovelace had all but torn off her nightclothes with his hot perusal. Best get everyone fed and back upstairs to the nursery, and perhaps hide there with them until after he'd gone off to bed.

She lifted the lid on the biscuit jar.

"The fits Cassandra threw when Mother told her she was delaying her come-out. I wanted to thrash her."

Mr. Lovelace murmured something inaudible.

Curiosity pulled her closer to the open door.

"Yes, I know," James said. "But after Charlotte arrived and Lady Glanford took us out to gather greenery, the girls ran about plotting and hanging kissing boughs everywhere."

"Cassandra said it's time for you to marry, and that you're going to marry Charlotte."

That plot had been obvious to everyone tonight. Mr. Lovelace remained silent. Perhaps he'd worked that out already. Perhaps he didn't mind and that's why he'd goaded her earlier about Charlotte.

"But Charlotte is too silly for you. Cassandra was fretting that you might like Lady Glanford better. I do. I think you should marry her."

Her heart thumped so loudly she almost missed the next words.

"Exthept, we don't have a feather to fly with."

The earthenware lid slipped, and she juggled it, almost dropping it.

Ben had heard the expression from one of their fellow travelers, and so tickled by the poetry of it, he'd searched out the meaning from a maid at the inn.

An argument erupted between the two Lovelace boys drowning out anything Mr. Lovelace might have said.

Clutching the sideboard, she steadied herself, letting the blood flow back to her hands. She really, really must stop eavesdropping.

Ben was only a child, and he wasn't intentionally trying to embarrass her.

And what did it matter what George Lovelace thought? She didn't want to marry—not him, or anyone else. Her boys were what mattered, protecting them, seeing to their futures.

She took a deep breath and returned to the biscuits. She'd tried to spare her boys the full truth. They couldn't have all they wished for, but they'd had all they needed in the way of food, good shoes, and proper clothing. And love. She'd made sure they knew they were loved.

"Do you want to argue, or do you want to hear about my railway?" Mr. Lovelace said, and the quarreling stopped.

Settling the lid on the jar, she hurried out. She would hear more about his railway. Never mind his arrogant leering. The railway might be a sound investment, once she had access to capital.

An embarrassed nursery maid appeared just as the boys finished another round of biscuits.

"Fell asleep, did you, Meg?" Mr. Lovelace teased.

"You know better, Master James and Master Edward," the middle-aged lady scolded, "sneaking about and bringing along the little one. Why you're as bad as..." She bit her lip and glanced at Mr. Lovelace, her eyes twinkling.

"Hah," James said. "As bad as George. And I'm too old to be in the nursery."

"Me too," Edward said.

"Off you all go," Sophie said before another argument started. "I'll tidy up here. Mr. Lovelace, would you accompany them and make sure there are no more disputes?"

He ushered them to the door. Her relief was cut short when she saw him returning.

"Please, Mr. Lovelace. Go. You must be tired after your journey."

He gathered up plates and mugs and she made herself shrug. "I suppose there's no point in arguing with you."

"None at all." He brushed by her, sending an unexpected tingle through her. "And by the way, my compliments on your boys. They are certainly better-behaved than my brothers."

"James and Edward have been very kind to my sons. I'm grateful."

"You don't find them too spirited?"

She thought of their green-gathering excursions and smiled. "Oh my, no. At home with family, children should be free to be spirited. Especially during the Yuletide."

"Perhaps their grief is easing. Father's death was hard on them."

"Yes. My condolences. I do understand."

He set down the cups and dishes. "Mother employs a scullery maid who will see to these. Come."

Tucking her hand over his arm, he pulled her into his warmth and they climbed the dark narrow stairs, the woodsy scent of his soap muddling her mind.

"Mother confided she's enjoying your visit. She likes a full nursery and I believe she's scheming. Not just about you sponsoring Miss Cartwright. She mentioned the boys. What are your plans for them when you go up to London? James and Edward will return to school. Perhaps Arthur could join them, and Ben can stay in the nursery with little Mary."

Send Arthur to school? The vicar had tutored him in Latin, and she herself was teaching both boys the other basics. But for the lack of funds, he was ready.

They climbed in silence to the second floor and paused on the landing. Dim light shone from a nearby lamp.

The thought of sending Arthur off depressed her. "At present, Arthur is being educated at home."

"He'll benefit from school," Mr. Lovelace murmured. "Not just from the instruction, but also from the connections and friendships."

She squeezed her eyes shut a moment and eased in a breath.

"I would miss him terribly, but I do agree, Mr. Lovelace. I..." Perhaps he might intervene with

Fitz. "I haven't yet had a chance to discuss schooling with your brother. As his mother, my decision-making is limited." As well as my means to pay school fees.

He frowned. "But...Glanford died over a year ago."

"Yes."

As his gaze searched her face, she tried to tame the turmoil inside her, reminding herself of Fitz's comment about Mr. Lovelace keeping her.

Warm hands enveloped her own and their grip firmed.

"Fitz hasn't spoken to you at all?"

She shook her head.

"Hasn't visited Arthur?"

"Not since Glanford's funeral. And thus, I am here. And it's late. I mean to rise early and shamelessly corner him over breakfast."

His thumbs swept over the backs of her hands, sending unexpected heat roaring through her.

"You are cold."

"Mr. Lovelace," she said, feeling breathless. "It's the middle of the night. I'm in the dark with a man, a man in his nightshirt and dressing gown, and he's fondling my hands. I am anything but cold at this moment."

His eyes lit, and the corners of his mouth quivered, and he bit back a grin. "My lady." He laughed. "Come this way." He tugged her a few steps and glanced up.

Her gaze followed his, and her heart turned cartwheels, pounding like the pistons of a steam engine. A treacherous kissing bough hung from the ceiling. This was a recent addition. She didn't remember the girls hanging it.

CHAPTER SEVEN

"Oh drat," she whispered. "Those girls." She stepped back and raised one of her hands, still engulfed in his.

The grin creasing his face made her knees weak. Before she could topple, he pulled her into his arms, cupped the back of her head, and she found herself looking up into midnight blue eyes and a silent request for permission.

The spark of attraction roared to a full blaze, sucking the air from her lungs. Her chin moved up and down of its own volition.

Softness. Warmth. The kiss was tender, almost tentative. His arm came around her and her breasts met hard muscle. She gasped, and his tongue touched hers, coaxing, convincing, melting her all the way to the soles of her feet, and then back up again. She'd been kissed before, quite thoroughly, but it had never stirred her like this.

He tugged her closer and her conscience whispered. Too many small ears and eyes about.

It was only a kiss—a passionate, determined, one but...Oh. His hand slid down to her backside and she gasped again.

If Glanford had ever aroused feelings like this...

Her heart took a leap and then crashed. Lovelace meant to seduce her. He was seeing how far she would let him go. No one had ever... They'd only just met, and he thought she would...

Blasted overbearing coxcomb.

She was calling his bluff. If he took this too far, one healthy scream would bring someone running.

She went up on her toes and matched him with lips and tongue and hands, threading her fingers through thick hair and—

He pulled away and rested his chin on the top of her head. His banyan had loosened, and her cheek touched warm skin and firm muscles.

Heavens. He was not wearing a nightshirt. And his heart was racing like a full team of horses.

***

With a huff, he loosened his embrace and Sophie slipped out of his arms, her glazed look moving from desire to confusion to...anger?

Would she clout him? Considering her answering kiss, that would be unjust.

Grinning, he crossed his arms.

"I shall avoid this spot on the landing," she said. "And don't try that behavior with Miss Cartwright."

"Miss Cartwright?" The girl was the furthest female from his mind. "Don't worry. She'll be like a sister to me. You, on the other hand..."

She leveled him with a heated gaze. "I, on the other hand, am not your sort."

"My sort?"

"I've no interest in a liaison. Not now and not if or when I bring Charlotte—Miss Cartwright—to town."

"You'll be staying with my brother. I'm bound to visit there during the season."

"And I am sure, you'll find plenty of ladies to court."

"What if I want to court you?"

"Don't mock. I'm not seeking a lover."

"What about a husband?"

"No. I have sons to guide and protect."

His mother must have made the same argument with herself about keeping James and Edward home for the term. But both ladies would sooner or later have to let go of the leading strings.

"In a year or two, they'll both be off and you'll go on with your life, seeing them during the school holidays. And though you're not perhaps in the first bloom of youth, you are still young enough, and quite beautiful, and—forgive my candor—gentlemen in need of heirs will note that you have produced two healthy sons."

Astonishment flashed, and the pulse in her neck started up. "I won't marry to serve as another nobleman's brood..." She bit her lip, her chest rising and falling most becomingly. "You are a provoking man, Lovelace, but I appreciate your bluntness. Let me be equally blunt. If I could find the sort of good man who'd be a proper stepfather to my boys, I have little to offer. You heard what my son Ben said."

"I did. A love match is not unheard of."

"Are you mad? What sort of love match could I find?" She shook her head, and hurried off down the corridor, hips swaying under the too short dressing gown.

Me. You could find me.

He followed her to a door where a maid appeared and looked him over appraisingly before ushering the lady in.

When the door latch clicked, he rubbed his eyes. Perhaps, like Fitz, he was also losing his mind.

The next morning, George entered the breakfast room to find only his mother.

She glanced up from a letter, wished him a good morning and sent the footman for fresh toast.

"I see I am late," he said. "Where is everyone?"

"Sophie took all the children out to gather more pine boughs and run off their exuberance. You can still catch up if you wish."

"Tempting," he said, surprised that he meant it. He turned away and busied himself filling a plate. Sophie's kiss had piqued more than his curiosity. He'd been up half the night thinking about her. "I'd best have a chat with Fitz first."

"Fitz left me a note. He's off to Melton Mowbray."

The tremor in her voice signaled anger. He seated himself next to her and unfolded the note she handed him. Fitz was leaving to join an impromptu hunting party and would return before the New Year.

Swallowing an oath, he accepted another letter and scanned the page. The candlemaker begged her ladyship's pardon, but would greatly appreciate payment of a debt months in arrears.

"I'm so happy you're home, my son." The hand patting his seemed frail. "I wonder if you might run into the village for me later. Perhaps talk to this merchant and run another small errand. The jeweler has resized a ring for me."

"I'd be happy to."

"The girls are planning to take the carriage today and shop."

"You're not going?"

"No. I'll send a maid and a footman."

Was Lady Glanford also going? He shook off the thought. Mother's concerns about Fitz came first.

And she must eat more. She was growing too thin.

When the footman returned, George heaped marmalade on toast and insisted she have some as well.

After their hunt for more greenery, Sophie left the younger children in the care of the nursery maids and went to tidy her hair. Not finding Fitz up yet, she'd agreed to the morning's expedition. The air had been thick with the smell of snow, and the footman who'd come along to help with the Yule log predicted it would begin falling before nightfall.

She found Willa at work picking out the hem of a crimson gown. The maid stood and shook out the dress. "Beautiful, ain't it?"

Sophie stripped off her gloves and lifted the lush silk. Seed pearls and blonde lace trimmed the neckline and hem, and the waistline and pouf sleeves were the latest in fashion.

"It's Lady Loughton's. Ordered last summer afore his lordship died. She said you must have it, as well as some day gowns she's put aside for you. Here." She pointed out a blue walking dress in a fine woolen cloth.

"I couldn't possibly."

"You've brought naught but two plain gowns, and those out of fashion. Better you look your best for Artie's sake. Let all know Lady Glanford means business."

She sighed. "All right. But don't ruin the cloth. She'll want those hems put back when we leave. Help me change out of these wet skirts."

"And you'll wear this blue wool today. 'Twill keep you warm and bring some blue to your eyes." Willa bustled about unlacing her. "And how are these stays? Biting too much?"

"They're fine."

"Hmm. We'll be having you looking your best. Bound to meet some of the neighbors in town today."

"In town?"

"I hear those girls planned to go into town."

"Oh yes, I did hear them mention it." Sophie fingered the cross at her neck. "Can you go with them and run an errand for me?"

"Aye. But won't you be going yerself?"

"I have to see Lord Loughton."

Willa went silent as she settled the blue gown over her, straightening it, and then sighing. "Lord Loughton's gone off this morning. Won't be back tonight."

"What?" Heat flooded her face. "G- gone off?"

"Off to Thurgood Manor near Melton Mowbray. Had it from the groom, Marty. Come and sit and I'll dress your hair." Willa held the dressing table chair for her. "Left a note for his mother. She was fit to be tied, they say, but that Mr. George Lovelace will have all in hand soon. Mayhap you should ask him for help?"

She dropped her gaze from the rising color reflected back at her in the mirror. Help from

George Lovelace might come at a higher price than a few kisses under the mistletoe.

Why did he stir her so?

"There." Willa patted her shoulder.

Sophie let out a breath. Willa had coaxed some of her thick mop into face-framing curls.

"Been wanting to do this," the maid said. "You look like yourself again. You'll catch some gentleman's—"

"Willa. You know I've no plans to marry." Once had been enough.

Sophie unhooked the chain at her neck and gazed again at her grandmother's cross. She'd told Glanford the metal was not real gold, that the garnets were just bits of glass, that it was merely a cheap family heirloom, dear for its memories. Only the last bit was true, but he'd believed her, and this piece of jewelry hadn't gone to pay creditors.

It will one day be yours and you may pass it to your own daughter, her mother had said.

Instead she'd had sons, and she was grateful for both of them. And they must have a Christmas.

"We may as well both go into town," she said.

The High Street was crowded with shoppers, and George greeted neighbors, thankful he hadn't spotted the ladies from Loughton Manor. He hurried past the drapers, where they might be thumbing through ribbons and bolts of cloth, and entered the jewelers.

Hawkins stood behind the counter frowning down at a short woman in a dark cape.

George raised a hand in greeting and studied a display of gold chains. With no other customers in the shop, he wouldn't have long to wait.

"I'm asking where you got it," Hawkins said.

"As I said," came the pleasant reply, "the cross is my lady's. I'm here at her behest to sell it. I've not stolen it."

"Perhaps you could fetch your lady to vouch for you."

"She's asked me to do this for her."

"I don't know you. Are you a visitor to these parts?"

The woman huffed out a breath. "I'm here for the sake of my lady's privacy."

George stepped closer.

"But, if you must know, we are guests—"

The floor creaked under him. The woman cast a glance back, and her mouth dropped open.

He barely managed to keep his from doing the same. He'd seen her in the doorway of Lady Glanford's bedchamber.

She bobbed a curtsy and reached for the item. Hawkins' hand came down, covering it, evoking a sputter of protest.

"Good day to you both." George joined them. "May I have a look, Hawkins?"

Hawkins lifted his hand revealing a gold cross set with garnets.

Color rose in the woman's wrinkled cheeks. Plump and older, she looked to be the sort of lady's maid who'd started as nurse to the woman she served.

"It's not stolen, Mr. Lovelace."

After an assessing look, more for Hawkins' sake than his own, he nodded. "I believe you." He turned the cross over. The initials inscribed on the back were not Lady Glanford's. Surely this was a family piece, and if it was the only jewelry she'd brought with her to Loughton Manor, it must be dear to her. "But, why is she selling it?"

He didn't need to ask, but he was curious to see the maid's response. One learned much about a man or woman from observing their servants.

She looked away, took a breath, and seemed to steel herself. "'Tis...'tis a private matter, sir. Meaning no disrespect."

"Of course." They hadn't a feather to fly with. "None taken. Hawkins, I'll vouch for this good woman. Carry on and I'll return later."

He stood in the haberdashery across the street, watching and thinking about the maid's quiet dignity, so like Sophie's. Was she the one who'd brought Sophie the news of her father's death?

All the shame of that day came back over him. Not all men were beastly to their wives. Father hadn't been, and neither were his brothers, not even Fitz. He ought to have spoken up more that day.

When Lady Glanford's maid exited the jewelers, he crossed the street and entered the shop.

After completing his mother's missions, he easily tracked the footman loading packages onto the family carriage. He pointed George to a shop that sold tea and sweets.

Cassandra beckoned him to a table she shared with Nancy, Miss Cartwright and Lady Glanford. "We've finished our cakes, George, but we'll sit with you while you have yours. Will you ride back with us in the carriage?"

"There's no room for me with all your packages, and it's a bracing fine day for a walk. And thank you, but I will pass on cakes."

"He's going to the inn to drink ale," Nancy said. "You never spend time with us anymore, George."

She sent Cassandra a sly look. "And we so wanted you to become acquainted with Charlotte."

Miss Cartwright's cheeks reddened like a late summer peach.

Lady Glanford stood. "Take my seat, Mr. Lovelace. I'll go now and see to the carriage."

Her maid appeared holding her cloak. Neither would look at him.

"The carriage is just outside, and I believe you should all climb in now, else Mother will be wondering if you've run off somewhere."

"Your brother is right," Lady Glanford said, urging them along.

"But you haven't shopped, Lady Glanford." Nancy said. "You haven't bought any gifts."

"And how could she with you along," George said. "You can't keep a secret to save yourself."

At the carriage, George handed the younger girls in while Lady Glanford held back.

When he offered her his hand, she shook her head. "I do have shopping to see to. Willa and I will walk back."

He cast a glance at the sky. After wading through the Loughton accounts, he'd needed the cold walk into town, but the weather had grown even colder and the state of the clouds meant the snow—when it came—would be heavy and fast.

"I will accompany you."

She blinked and opened her mouth.

"Your maid—Willa is it? Willa must ride back in the carriage. Willa, I shall see to your lady's safe arrival home, no matter the weather."

Lady Glanford cast a glance at the maid.

"I insist. Willa, you appear to be a woman of great good sense. I'm trusting you to keep my nodcock sisters and Miss Cartwright in hand." He took the maid's arm, helped her in, and closed the door.

"Now," he said. "Your shopping. Gifts for Arthur and Ben, is it?"

"Sir, you needn't trouble yourself—"

"I happen to know where to buy the best toys."

"There is no need. Your sisters have led me through every shop on and off the high street."

"Oh, but you'll need someone to carry your packages." He set her hand upon his arm. "Let us try to finish before the snow starts."

***

As they left the village, the snow began falling in earnest, gathering on the brim of Mr. Lovelace's hat and in the folds of Sophie's red mantle, and cloaking the stark grays and browns of the winter landscape.

Elation bubbled up in her and she laughed. "The snow is magical, isn't it? The boys will love this. But I suppose we'd best hurry." She stepped out, and stumbled.

Strong arms caught her, steadying her against a firm chest, reminding her of the kiss under the mistletoe.

She took in a jittery breath and with it, the scent of clean starch and a man's bergamot cologne that started her trembling.

"Come," he said. "You're cold. Let's turn back. I'll borrow a carriage."

CHAPTER EIGHT

Sophie squeezed her eyes shut and eased in another breath. They'd spent a companionable hour in town. Mr. Lovelace, as it turned out, shopped the way she liked to, when she was able: quickly and decisively, haggling only as needed to reach a fair agreement for both parties.

For James and Edward, she'd bought carved flutes, Mr. Lovelace assuring her the nursery staff wouldn't curse her for the noisy gifts. For little Mary, she'd found a tiny reticule; for the older girls and Lady Loughton, handkerchiefs she'd find time to embroider; for Willa, a skein of yarn for a scarf; for Ben, some toy soldiers; and for Artie, a spyglass.

Artie's gift had been surprisingly affordable—suspiciously so. In the midst of negotiations, the shopkeeper's proud wife had enticed Sophie away to see a chubby new grandbaby. Mr. Lovelace had concluded the transaction.

It had been kind of him. She would pay him back whatever extra he'd paid after she visited Papa's jeweler in London.

Mr. Lovelace had also introduced her to other merchants and neighbors who'd greeted her warmly. No one pulled her aside asking when she would pay her bill or repair the fences. Though, she recollected, the chandler had scurried out of his shop for a whispered discussion with Mr. Lovelace. She wondered if Lady Loughton was in arrears, and if so, why? Were the Lovelaces in financial straits? If so, what might it mean for her boys? So many worries.

But the snow...the snow was magical, spreading a white blanket over broken bricks, ruts in the road, and overgrown hedges. The snow made everything beautiful.

"Are you well?" he murmured into her ear.

She blinked back sudden moisture. Lured her onto a balcony and one stumble later...

She'd stumbled into another man's arms. Oh, but this man was so...so...solid. And warm.

He smoothed a hand down her back, sending her heart into a rapid tattoo.

No life there...Like bedding the dead...need to marry money...find you another bumbling long Meg with a purse...get her to stumble into you.

She stepped back. George Lovelace's eyes were warm, and laugh lines crinkled his face, reminding her he'd come away laughing from that conversation with Glanford. He must have gone on laughing for many years.

She shook off the ugly memory. She'd made up her mind to forget. Through the weeks after Papa's death, the months of her confinement, and the hours of childbirth, she'd churned over the words spoken that day. But with her first view of Artie, she set her mind to her fate.

She was a countess with a son who needed her. She'd tried harder. She'd found a circle of kind acquaintances. And when she'd finally allowed Glanford back into her bed, it was on her terms. Fortunately, after Ben's birth, he'd mostly left her alone.

He touched her arm. "Have you twisted your ankle, my dear?"

The blasted man was too kind. "I'm fine."

"Take my arm. We'll go back to the inn and borrow horses."

Her equestrian skills had been another marital disappointment.

"I'm not dressed for riding."

"A carriage or cart then."

She straightened her spine, determined to match his courtesy. "It's not long until dinner. We can walk in less time than it will take to arrange transport." She brushed snow from her bonnet. "And I do love the snow. Such a welcome change from rain. Run along and hire yourself a horse. I intend to walk."

"A gentleman wouldn't—"

"Don't be silly. You've arranged for my purchases to be delivered, so I'm not lugging packages, and I'm perfectly capable of walking a mile by myself. Besides, I'd not wish to be the cause of ruining your boots."

He gazed down at her feet. "And what of yours?"

"They've withstood worse."

One dark eyebrow rose.

Fine. They were the worse for that wear, but never mind. Her boys' boots were sturdy and new, and that was what mattered.

"Go then." She shooed him and stepped out.

Footsteps crunched next to her as he caught up, pulling her hand over his arm.

"I take it you're one of those country ladies who tramps about through the fields with her dogs."

"I walk, certainly." She'd escaped at every chance when Glanford was underfoot.

"Except when your coachman is driving you about. That is more my mother's style."

She focused on the road, ignoring the teasing kindness. They'd dispensed with the coach and the coachman even before Glanford's death.

"Or you drive out in your own gig," he mused.

"I've never been much of a whip."

"No? Well then, you had the company of your dogs, perhaps. A great pack of them, like the Duchess of York?"

"Glanford had hounds." He'd lavished more attention on them than his family.

"You had no lap dog?" he teased. "No giant mongrel standing guard?"

They'd reached the turn for Loughton Manor. She freed her hand and passed through the gate ahead of him.

"Neither," she said. Much as Glanford loved his hounds, he'd banned the sort of pets that would have brought comfort to the boys or warmth to her bed...a dog or a cat or two.

He touched her arm, stopping her.

"I've offended you. Or..."

He gazed down at her, not quite frowning. She took a step back, quelling her rising anger.

Damn the man. She didn't need his pity.

"I've raised bad memories. How thoughtless of me." He stepped closer, backing her off the lane, into a sheltered patch between a large showy yew and the boundary wall.

"Lady Glanford. I've been wanting...want to...to apologize."

Her pulse pounded in her ears. This close, she could see the spiky late afternoon stubble peppering his cheeks. She curled her fingers in, resisting the temptation to touch, gathering her composure.

"For the kiss, Mr. Lovelace? It was nothing."

He blinked. "No. That is, I wanted to say how sorry I am about the scene in the Townsends' garden so many years ago."

A dull ache started up near her heart and she felt her color rising under his warm gaze.

Drat the man. She wasn't that young girl anymore. She'd withstood the disgrace. She'd weathered the whispers. The past mustn't matter. It was the present that must concern her.

"Apology accepted." As she pushed by, he snatched her hand and the hard planes of his face softened.

"Thank you. I've always been ashamed I didn't—"

"What? Confront Glanford?" She inched away, catching her breath as a branch poked her back.

"Defend you. Especially after I heard your father had just—"

"Stop." She yanked her hand away and fought a surge of tears. For months she'd grieved Papa's death and her miserable marriage. Her boys had saved her, and now she must save them. Noble they might be, like their father, but they'd have the good sense of common Englishmen.

Glanford had run through Papa's hard-earned money at a dizzying pace and then somehow got his hands on her dower and Ben's trust as well. If Papa had lived... But he hadn't. And now she had only the boys' guardian to help her, a man who wouldn't answer her letters or speak to her.

"You have no need to take on my husband's shame." She gritted her teeth. "On the other hand, there's the matter of your brother's."

His mouth turned down into a guarded frown. "He's dishonored you?"

"Dishonored?" She blinked. Then scoffed. "Dishonored me? Fitz? No, he hasn't dishonored me in that way." Her hands curled into fists as she struggled for breath. "He's been dishonorable in other ways. He's dishonored his duty, to my sons. Fitz...Fitz is like Glanford. A...a ramshackle, cork-brained booby."

His gaze narrowed on her, his lips firming into a white line. Indignation or anger?

At her?

She straightened her spine. Good. The stinger had hit home. He was too much the gentleman to strike her, but he'd defend his beastly brother. Didn't she always tell her own sons to stand together?

"My brother," he said in a tight voice, "lost his wife and newborn son. He's not been the same since."

And what of my boys?

She eased in a breath. "Yes. One must have an excuse."

His eyes sparked. "He did love her. I've watched him struggle with the loss of a beloved spouse, just as my mother is struggling. Neither of us knows what that's like."

Her throat thickened again, her cheeks heating. "Touché, Mr. Lovelace." She held his gaze, trying to master her rising anger. "However, we both know what it is to lose a parent. Surprising it might be, but my boys, like your brothers, loved their father. But they don't have four older brothers to rely upon. They have only me, and a guardian who is a malingering shirker."

She stepped to the side and he matched her, grasping her shoulders.

"You're angry." His voice shook, low and dangerous, and he tugged her into an embrace, her ear pressed to his pounding heart. "You're not in this alone. I will help you."

His hand smoothed along her back, stirring his words into mayhem within her. She wasn't alone? He would help her? What was the cost? There was always a cost.

Would she mind paying it?

She lifted her head and stared up at him. "How?"

His gaze sent heat unfurling in tiny bursts along her skin, drawing her lips like a magnet.

A man has to make some effort. What does my pup of a brother know about bed sport? Lovelace had learned something over the years. He stirred her with no more than his essence and an effortless look.

It was intoxicating. Perhaps she wouldn't mind... Oh.

His lips touched hers, and she yielded, head spinning, nerves heating and firing, heart pounding out of her chest. She bumped the stone wall, and he spun them around, bracing himself there and pulling her into him.

Her fingers threaded his thick hair and knocked off his hat, while she drowned in the feel of his hands sliding under her cloak, over her back, her breasts, her bottom. Pleasure flooded her, heady and potent, like nothing she'd ever felt before.

She heard herself moan, and he lifted his head.

"Sophie?" He whispered the question, his eyes dark as midnight.

She blinked, still befuddled. What was he asking?

The corner of his lip quirked, and he found a spot on her neck. His warm kiss sent shivers through her.

"Yes," she said. Yes, yes, yes. Don't stop.

Eyes glittering, he smiled and drew her impossibly, close, their hearts beating together. Abandoning her lips, he dropped kisses along her cheek, paused to savor her neck and moved on to the top of her bodice.

Her hand traveled over his wide shoulders and firm chest and down to his trousers until she felt the hard length of him.

And he froze.

***

"Shhh," George said, more to his own pounding heart than to Lady Glanford. He'd heard a noise. They must take this somewhere more private.

Her bedchamber or his? She had a maid—so, his. Could they get past the gauntlet of family and servants? Could they stay there all night without being discovered?

A sound drifted again through the dense air: crunching footsteps, giggling, boys' voices.

Sophie lifted her head and looked over her shoulder. "Oh dear."

Gad, if the boys had discovered them... "We're well-hidden," he murmured.

She nodded and looked away. "I...I shouldn't have allowed that. Not that you seemed to have minded."

"Nor you, Sophie. May I call you that?"

She lifted a shoulder. "That was...well, I thank you, but we mustn't go down this path again, Mr. Lovelace."

"Call me George. You call my brother by his Christian name."

"Only because he visited Glanford so often. I...I have to think of the boys."

They would go down this path again. He'd make certain of it.

He set her back from him, straightened her bonnet and returned to the lane to fetch his own hat.

A hard mass of snow smacked his cheek like an icy cudgel and he heard Sophie's gasp.

"Get back, Sophie." He clamped his hat on. "Boys. Let Lady Glanford pass in peace."

Loud giggling drifted through the dense air. Snow pelted his forehead knocking his hat askew.

Sophie's cloak brushed him in passing. She ducked, scooping up great handfuls of snow. "Come out, come out, wherever you are," she shouted.

A blizzard exploded against her red cloak. She launched her volleys in rapid succession, and a shriek pierced the air.

"You rapscallions won't win this," she taunted.

Another snowball struck the side of her head, and she gasped, laughing.

"Let the lady pass." George swooped her behind a bush. "I've spotted four of them. I fear my brothers are corrupting your sons."

"Nonsense." She righted herself and scooped up more snow. "Artie and Ben love a good snowball fight. Come, George. We shall make a good team."

He and Sophie, a team?

He laughed. "You'll regret this, boys."

"We won. We beat you, Mama." Ben grinned as Sophie mopped his wet head.

"Four against two," James said. "We were bound to win."

George caught the twinkle in Sophie's eye.

Like the others, she'd shed her wet cape and boots at the kitchen entrance. Her damp skirts clung enticingly, and locks of hair tumbled around her shoulders.

"We shall have a rematch," George said. "But not today. It's time for your dinner, and Lady Glanford is soaked to the bone."

"I'm only a little damp," she said. "As are you. Please go on up, Mr. Lovelace."

"I'll wait for you."

She pulled a face at him. "A rematch is a fine idea, boys. We'll ask your sisters and Charlotte and Mary to join in."

That launched a debate about uneven teams, interrupted by the appearance of two nursery maids, who escorted the boys in a noisy cavalcade up the backstairs.

Sophie would have gone with them, but he pulled her aside. "We didn't finish our conversation before the battle."

Her cheeks flamed. "Best that we say no more on the subject, Mr. Lovelace."

He glanced toward the servants' hall. They were quite out of view. "George. And it's not a conversation requiring words."

She raised an eyebrow. "You are speaking of criminal conversation?"

"Of course not. Neither of us is married."

A long moment ensued while she drew herself up and cloaked herself with icy composure. As the moment stretched, his spirits rose.

Her shoulders sagged and she let out a long breath. "No. There must be no distracting entanglements."

She turned away, and he hurried after her. This wasn't over. He'd only begun the siege. If she traveled to London, he'd find a way. If she returned to Lancashire, well, even better.

In the entry hall, they met the butler on his way to answer the front door.

"Visitors?" Sophie halted and patted her hair. "I look a fright. I'll go back and make my way up by the servants' stairs."

He drew her aside into an alcove. "Nonsense. You look beautiful. Full of life. A countess lively enough to engage in a snow fight."

"You're talking flummery, Mr. Lovelace."

"Call me 'George'."

"I only hope I don't embarrass your mother with this caller."

The man Biggs ushered in was a stranger. Of medium height and sturdy build, he handed a footman his caped greatcoat and beaver hat and gave orders about his trunk.

George approached and greeted him.

"Lord Loughton?" His gaze slid over the damp coats and trousers and down to his wet stocking-feet, then shifted to Sophie. He blinked, and frowned.

"No sir, I'm George Lovelace, Lord Loughton's brother. And you are...?"

"Beg pardon." He extended his hand. "I'm Cartwright, Charlotte's father. Lady Loughton offered me hospitality, should I be able to get away for the Yuletide."

Thus, the fine clothing, face like a prize-fighter's, and direct manner.

"I see. Well, welcome. And, may I introduce another guest, Lady Glanford?"

Sophie executed a dignified curtsy.

"Lady Glanford." He frowned. "Lady Loughton wrote to me about you."

"Yes, I know," she said. "It's a pleasure to meet you. And now, I fear I must go up directly. Mr. Lovelace and I were caught out in the snow. Good day to you, sir."

Her words had been smooth, but she stumbled upon the second stair.

George bowed. "I'll leave you in the capable hands of our butler. It's almost time to dress for dinner. I hope we may talk more then."

He caught up with Sophie and they went up together.

At the landing, she glanced up at the kissing bough and stepped out of his reach. Her gaze slid to the stairs. "Well that is that," she whispered.

"What is what? What are you talking about?"

She grimaced. "He doesn't remember me. He called on my father once. I shall not be shepherding his daughter about London."

"I haven't understood why you would want to."

"I have business in London."

"So have your man see to it, or Fitz..."

Her lips firmed in a determined frown. "This business doesn't involve Fitz."

George rubbed his jaw. "Who has been no help to you anyway." He stepped closer and took her hand. "As I said, I will help you. I can see to your business in London if Cartwright spurns you, but I can't imagine why he would."

She raised an eyebrow and swept a hand over her person. "Would you put your young daughter in the care of a woman who looks like this?"

She looked beautiful and fresh and alive. He'd put himself into her care in a heartbeat.

But perhaps she had a point. She was far too desirable to serve as a chaperone.

Biggs's voice floated up the staircase. He'd be escorting Cartwright up soon.

George ushered her down the corridor, closer to her bedchamber. "You've been caught out in the weather. He'll understand."

"He's a competent businessman, like my father was. He'll already have made inquiries about me. He'll know I'm the daughter of Wardell Clark, not a born lady. He'll know about Glanford. All strikes against me perhaps. And I've made an untidy first impression."

He tucked a lock of hair behind her ear. "He'll think what any man will think. That you're beautiful."

A mulish look came over her. "I must go to London. A few weeks of parties and social events seemed a small price to pay. I must help myself, and London has always been part of that scheme. Fitz has been useless."

"Sophie," he said, moving close enough to catch her flowery scent. "I'm not useless."

Her bedchamber door opened. "Begging your pardon, sir," her maid said, "but my lady needs to get out of these wet clothes before she catches her death."

George escorted her to the door, promised to speak more with her later, and then found his way to his own room.

What was she seeking in London? Despite her claims, was she after another husband?

He tore off his damp coats, fighting the urge to go pound on her door and ask.

A pile of post caught his eye and he went to it. His brother Selwyn's letter would offer Christmas greetings and a report on investments. The Duke of Kinmarty would write about his son's first tooth or some such—he'd taken up fatherhood with a vengeance.

The third letter was from his business partner. He opened it.

Dear Lovelace,

I hope this finds you and your family well. I write from London, where I've encountered both progress and setbacks. I shall start with the infelicitous news first.

Regrettably, Lord Stanley's support for our railway bill is faltering. Your brother's active sponsorship is essential. Please write to me of his assurances, as I will be pursuing other votes for the bill being presented this session.

Happily, I have confirmed that our mysterious right-of-way property holder may have been found. As we suspected, ownership had indeed changed hands, quietly, and with the deed not properly recorded. All this from the clerk who would not make free with the name yet, only to say that his master had written to the new owner's guardian and received no reply. He also advised that the steward overseeing the minor's estate said the family (precisely, the minor's mother, an obdurate widow) was known to oppose any use of the land that would sully the pristine acres. I shall continue to press the matter, and ask that you travel to Lancashire to investigate and track down the parties involved.

Please convey my warmest Yuletide greetings to Lady Loughton and Lord Loughton.

With kindest regards, etc.
J. Ellison

He paced to the window. The snowfall had ceased, and the sky had cleared, a bright moon lighting this pristine landscape.

Magical, she'd called it.

The kissing that followed had certainly been magical. The snowball fight as well. The lady had gone from proper, to passionate, to playful in three beats of his heart. If she returned to her home instead of traveling to London, he would escort her. Glanford's estate was in Lancashire.

He scanned the letter again.

A guardian who didn't answer letters, a widow, an owner quietly gaining title to land...

In payment of a gambling debt, perhaps?

Could it be? Ninety-nine times out of a hundred, the late Lord Glanford had held the losing hand.

The dinner gong sounded, and he hastened to dress, anxious to see her.

He'd promised to help her. He'd spent the morning in the study going over the Loughton accounts. After dinner, he must see what documents Fitz was holding about young Glanford's estate.

CHAPTER NINE

Seated down the table from Sophie, George caught only snippets of her conversation with Cartwright.

She'd been the last to appear for dinner, but she'd used the time preparing well. The daring green gown sported beadwork and lace that made up for her lack of jewelry. Tonight, a wide ribbon circled her neck in lieu of the garnet cross. Cartwright, the bounder, eyed her bosom while he interrogated her about her acquaintances in town.

From this distance, her murmured replies sounded calm, almost bored.

She'd hidden away the warm, feeling, lively woman. What a pity she felt she must act out a role in his family home all to secure a means of traveling to London.

"You're very quiet, Mr. Lovelace," Miss Cartwright said.

"He's ignoring your attempts at conversation." Nancy smirked at him.

"I beg your pardon, Miss Cartwright."

"The snowball fight knocked the stuffing out of you I heard." Nancy giggled. "It was so unfair you didn't invite us."

"What is this about a snowball fight?" Cartwright called, proof the man was doing his own bit of eavesdropping.

Cartwright glanced at Sophie. "Is that where you'd both come from?"

Sophie smiled at her half-empty plate. "One has to make the best of a snowy day."

Cartwright glanced at her and then down the table at George. "You engaged Lady Glanford in a snowball fight?"

Mother laughed. "George would never attack a lady. They were walking back from the village when they were set upon. I do hope there are no stuffed-up noses and sore throats in the nursery."

"Your younger sons were involved, my lady?" Cartwright directed the question to Mother.

"Yes."

"They sound like a jolly lot." He put down his fork.

"And you will meet them tonight." Mother stood, bringing everyone to their feet. "The ladies and I will enjoy our dessert in the drawing room where the children will join us. Mr. Cartwright, George you may remain here, if you wish."

Remaining behind would only embroil him in a conversation with Cartwright and delay his business in the study. "Let's go along, Cartwright. You can't top this bunch for jolliness. I'll bring the bottle of port."

"Do come, Papa," Charlotte said.

"Very well." Cartwright pushed back his chair. "And perhaps you and I can chat, Lovelace."

He swallowed his annoyance and said, "Of course."

In the drawing room, servants carried in trays. George led Cartwright to a gaming table and poured their drinks.

"I've heard tell you're building a railway, Lovelace."

George eyed him over the rim of his glass. Their plans weren't exactly confidential—certainly wouldn't be when Parliament got involved, but his corporation wasn't the only group seeking to build. Cartwright might be part of a budding competition.

While he picked over how much information to reveal, the nursery crew arrived and headed for the sweets.

"What is your interest?" George asked.

Cartwright smiled, then laughed. "Same as yours. Making money. Vulgar to say, perhaps, but there it is."

"George." Mother shooed the children toward him. "Make introductions please."

Cartwright's mouth dropped open. "Four younger brothers?"

"No. Those two are my brothers James and Edward." George rested one hand on Arthur's shoulder and the other atop Ben's head. "And this is Arthur, Lord Glanford, and his brother, Ben."

A maid brought over a tray with an assortment of sweets and hurried off.

Cartwright patted his stomach. "After that excellent dinner, I'll wait. Dive in, young ones."

James and Edward snatched up treats and hurried away. Arthur helped his young brother with a plate, then filled his own and turned to go.

"It's no wonder Charlotte is happy here. Generous of your mother to host her and Lady Glanford, as well. A pity Glanford was such a wastrel."

Arthur's thin shoulders froze. He turned around, back straight, plate tilting and threatening to lose its sweets.

"Sir." He pinned the older man with a glare. "That is my father you're speaking of."

Cartwright's eyes glinted with keen interest.

Color rose in the boy's cheeks and his eyes—so like his mother's—darkened. "We don't speak ill of him, nor do we countenance others doing so."

George let out a breath, watching the duel. He could imagine those words coming from Sophie's mouth, and with the same expression of dignified ire.

Cartwright held the boy's gaze a long moment, then dipped his head. "Quite right," he said evenly. "The good book tells us: Honor thy father and thy mother. Keep to the good book and you'll grow into a good man, and a good earl, as well." He extended his hand. "Accept my apologies?"

Arthur shook his hand and ran off.

Perhaps he could do business with Cartwright. As Sophie had pointed out, a project like theirs could never have too much money.

"Well, well," Cartwright mused. "Defending his father's honor, no matter how thinly it was spread. I'd wager that's his mother's doing. Clark always valued loyalty. He'd be proud. Seems his daughter has become the true lady he always wanted her to be."

The lady in question was ruffling through song sheets at the pianoforte. She hadn't witnessed the scene.

"A handsome woman, isn't she?" Cartwright said, watching her.

Jealousy reared in him. Chaperoning Charlotte would throw Cartwright and Sophie together. If she truly was penniless...

He'd promised to help her, and he would. "Cartwright, I've some correspondence to see to. I'm afraid it can't wait. Please feel free to avail yourself of my brother's library."

"And you'll owe me that chat," Cartwright called after him.

He bowed and made good his escape.

***

Sophie said her goodnights and escorted the children, leaving them in the care of the nursery maid. In her bedchamber, she found Willa stitching the hem of a dress.

"Not another one." Lady Loughton's generosity was out of hand.

"Aye." She held up the royal blue sarcenet and got to her feet. "This was from last year. Said she'd only worn it but the once. Ready to turn in?"

"No. Go on to bed. I shall manage when I return."

"You're going somewhere? Wake me, as you won't manage those hooks without help."

She'd hate for anything to spoil the lovely green gown. "Perhaps I'll change into my old morning dress."

Willa turned her around and began unhooking her. "Where are you off to? In case that you don't return and I need to go looking."

"You won't need to go looking."

Willa paused. "You're not visiting Mr. Love—"

"Of course not. Why would you think that?"

"Hmm. I did happen to peek out of the door late last night. And then you came back with him, both of you soaked, and there's that bruise on your neck I covered with the ribbon."

Her hand flew to the spot where he'd kissed her that afternoon.

The maid chuckled.

"I'm not meeting anyone. I hope everyone has turned in. I'm going to search Lord Loughton's study, and I pray Mr. Lovelace won't be there."

"Pity. He might do you a world of good."

"Willa. I won't risk my reputation."

"He might want to marry you."

"He doesn't. He's a full five years younger than me. Gentlemen like him want young women with good childbearing prospects and a healthy dowry."

"Maybe. Maybe not."

Sophie stepped out of the gown and rubbed her side where the stays were digging.

"Let me loosen those. Or you might take them off altogether. I'll guard them well."

She trusted her maid above all others. And yet...

She reached for her old gown. "No. I must hurry."

"You know, my dear, Mr. Lovelace ain't the heir. There's five other brothers and any one of them might father a boy. In any case you've had two and you're not too old for another. He may be younger but he's plenty old enough to be thinking of marriage. And he's not poor. He could help you."

She squeezed her eyes shut. Glanford had married her only for money. No way would she turnabout and pursue Lovelace for the same mercenary reasons.

"Downstairs speak well of him."

Ignoring the maid, she went to light a candle. "Don't wait up."

"Sure and you don't want me? Two extra hands make for a faster job."

"I wouldn't risk you getting caught."

"By who? His lordship is gone...Ah." Willa turned away, but not before Sophie saw her sly smile.

"Stop, Willa. The house is quiet. He'll have gone up."

"Hmm. Might be another kissing bough in the study."

"Aargh. Go to bed."

As she slipped into the corridor, the door closed on Willa's deep chuckle.

Inside the study, an Argand lamp shone brightly on a pair of expensive shoes propped on the desk.

Drat and double drat.

Mr. Lovelace—George—tossed aside a newspaper and stood, coming around the desk and crossing the thick Aubusson carpet.

"Sophie." He tilted his head, examining her. "Is anything wrong?"

"Other than your brother's continued absence?"

His mouth firmed. "Mr. Cartwright questioned you rather closely during dinner."

"And well he should. We'll see what else he's curious about when we have our private interview."

He straightened. "Private?"

"We've yet to negotiate the more unrefined part of the arrangement—my compensation. We shall see what he wants to pay me and what he expects to get for it."

A deeper frown settled over George. He felt some antipathy toward Mr. Cartwright. Was it a matter of class, or something else?

"As long as the unrefinement only involves a discussion of money for chaperoning Charlotte."

Oh. She let out a breath. Might he be jealous? Perhaps their two kisses had him feeling possessive.

She wanted to laugh, but decided to take her own jab at him. "He had you pulled aside after dinner, didn't he? Worried you'll offer for Charlotte?"

"Gad, no. He's interested in my railway."

"Does he wish to invest? He's very rich."

"Perhaps. Or else he's nosing about for our competitors."

"Or perhaps he wants to make your iron rails? Who have you contracted with?"

His lip quirked. "Are you spying for Cartwright?"

"If it's worth my while, I might be willing to act as his agent. Perhaps he and I may discuss it after we speak about Charlotte's come-out."

"I will be present for any such conversation."

"Really, Mr. Lovelace."

"George."

She threw up her hands. "George. Your mother will be present and she can report back to you."

As she slipped by him, his arm came around her shoulder.

"Fair enough, Sophie. Now, why this unexpected visit in the middle of the night? Were you looking for me?"

"No. I was hoping you wouldn't be here."

His chuckle tickled her ear.

"I'm looking for information."

"About the guardianship?"

"Yes. And the Glanford accounts."

"Your steward—"

"Won't tell me anything, as I have no legal authority, he says. Though I am the one the tenants confide in. If only we might buy new equipment, and adopt newer methods of farming..."

"You're involved in the estate management?"

"I would like to be. I've come to enjoy the countryside, and to care for the people."

He turned her around to face him. "Mother said you sent letters."

"I did. Fitz hasn't answered them, and I made sure they were posted."

He clenched his jaw, his dark look returning. "All I've found are the guardianship papers. I've looked in every cabinet, and box, and drawer." He grimaced and walked back to the desk. "Except this one. It's locked."

She moved up next to him. "You don't have a key?"

"I have several but none of them work."

"May I?" She brushed by him, shoved back the chair, and bent down, examining the lock.

His quick intake of breath and the chuckle that followed sent hot blood to her cheeks and made her drop to her knees. "Let's pick the lock, Mr. Lovelace."

"Call me George." When she looked up, a small smile curved his lips and his gaze had darkened.

"Not when you look at me that way." She drew out a pin, and tucked the dislodged lock of hair behind her ear. "Well?"

"By all means. How did you learn your criminal skills?"

"One develops talents when one is kept in the dark."

"Indeed," he said, sounding thoughtful.

Shushing him, she put her ear to the lock. His closeness sent her heart pounding and her thoughts straying to that last kiss.

With a deep breath, she steadied her hand.

"Shall I try?" His breath tickled her ear.

"Mr. Lovelace. Please."

Chuckling, he seated himself, the chair creaking under him, his knees bumping her shoulder.

She froze. George stilled as well. The creaking continued.

Heavy steps thudded across the carpet.

"Cartwright." George called.

She squeezed herself into the desk's kneehole and tried not to breathe.

CHAPTER TEN

"Thought you would have gone up," George said too loudly.

The guest chair thumped, and George shifted closer. The scents of wood polish and shoe leather filled her nose, and she squeezed back a sneeze.

"Fine library Loughton has here." The older man's deep rumble permeated the heavy mahogany. "Thought I might go up, and then I saw your candle moving this way."

Oh Hades. He'd seen her candle. She'd nearly been caught.

"I see you've got the Manchester paper there from last week. I read the piece on the new Stockton and Darlington Railway bill."

George's shoe bumped her as he shifted again, and she pressed her cheek to the cool mahogany, holding her breath, barely hearing his murmured reply to Cartwright. The closeness was addling her, and he was fidgeting like Ben did when he was practicing his letters.

When his knee nudged her shoulder, she teetered and reached for the nearest brace—his leg. The solid muscle flinched under her fingers.

Breathless again, she pressed her cheek to his knee and swallowed a surge of longing. What would it be like to make love to a man she wanted?

Easing in a breath, she tried to still her racing heart and the temptation threatening to overtake her.

George emitted a strangled cough and cleared his throat. "Cartwright. Tell me more about your interest in the railway."

"I've heard rumors it's a grand plan. I might want to invest, if you're selling shares."

George shifted, and her hand moved of its own accord sliding up the firm muscle, venturing higher to the bend of his knee.

A sharp intake of breath rattled through him.

Cartwright laughed. "I'm not a competitor, I can assure you of that. You think on it and we can talk more in the light of day. Now, perhaps you might tell me what you know of Lady Glanford. Fetching woman, isn't she? Your mother is pushing hard for her to manage Charlotte's come-out, but I'm not so sure Lady Glanford won't be turning heads herself. Not that she'd compete with my Charlotte for offers of marriage of course, but—"

"Cartwright." George's chair jerked back taking him with it. "We might as well discuss the railway now. Come, let's go to the library where the chairs are more comfortable."

Sophie lolled back and clamped a hand over a mad giggle. She'd rattled the oh-so-sure-of-himself Mr. Lovelace. Who knew he could be such a coward?

Or that she could be so wicked?

No...not wicked. That had been foolish.

When she heard the sharp click of the door, she crawled out and returned to her criminal enterprise.

***

It was past midnight when Cartwright finally went off to bed and George hastened back to the study hoping Sophie was waiting for him.

Her intentions were clear. The only question to answer was: his bedchamber or hers?

He found her at the desk bent over a letter. Other correspondence sat stacked on each side of the desktop.

He silently closed the door. "What did you find?"

She stood and paced to the fireplace, worrying her hands at her waist.

"Sophie? What did you find, my dear?"

Her fingers rubbed her temples. "It is worse than I feared. I thought I could... I'd hoped..." She squeezed her eyes shut. "I must think."

He went to her and took her hands. "I said I will help you, and I will. We'll find a way."

She lifted her chin, but there was no defiance in it, and he couldn't read the emotion in her eyes.

"You have worries of your own. I will have to find my way to London as soon as possible, after I speak with Fitz."

"You're not going with Cartwright."

She searched his face. "What?"

After thirty minutes probing George for information about Sophie, and one man to another, making his interest clear, Cartwright had mentioned he'd travel to London before the New Year.

"You can't serve as Charlotte's sponsor."

She let out a tight breath and pulled her hands away. "He knew I was under the desk."

Had Cartwright known? "No. He's..." Looking for a lover. George reached for her hand again, watching annoyance play on her face. "Sophie, I'm not entirely sure his intentions toward you are honorable."

She scoffed. "Then you are two peas in the same pod." Her lips pressed together. "I apologize for my earlier forwardness. Be assured I'm not going to London as anyone's mistress. That sort of business enterprise doesn't interest me at all."

He held her gaze deciding whether to laugh or to chastise. She'd just been on her knees in an enterprising position. And the kisses that afternoon and the night before had not been produced by an uninterested woman.

"Do not worry," she said. "I understand men like Cartwright far better than I do the genteel sort, and if I chaperone Charlotte, I'll make my intentions clear."

When she wasn't hiding under a desk or standing under the mistletoe, Sophie had principles. She wouldn't take a carte blanche from the man.

Oh hell. The way Cartwright had spoken of her, he might...he might...

His jaw tightened. "He might want marriage."

"Marriage?"

"Yes."

"To me?"

"It's not so outlandish."

"I don't wish to marry. I've been married, Lovelace. I fulfilled my marriage contract. I did my marital duty, and my duty didn't end with Glanford's death. I have children, and tenants, and a community that depend on me."

"You're not going to London to seek a husband?"

"Are you daft?" She sniffed his breath. "Or...foxed. You've been drinking."

He pressed his forehead to hers. "I'm not drunk, Sophie. I'm..."

I'm in love.

Head spinning, he pulled her into a kiss. He wanted her. She should be his.

She broke the kiss and touched his cheek, and then yanked her hand away. "I have children. You have a railway. We can't do this." Her eyes glistened betraying her lie.

"We can."

Lips trembling, she looked away. "Perhaps one day. Not now. I have responsibilities."

The longing in her voice stirred his spirits. "One day, then." Tomorrow, if he had his way. He tucked a lock of hair behind her ear. "Now, what did you find?"

"Letters. The stack on the right had been opened." She squeezed her eyes shut. "The file in the middle contains IOUs. Glanford owed Fitz an ungodly amount."

She stepped out of his arms and returned to the desk, collecting the opened letters.

"May I read those?" George asked.

"Tomorrow. I need to study them tonight, and I'll leave them for you in the morning."

More letters were piled on a corner of the desk. "What is this other correspondence?"

"See for yourself. I'm going up."

He reached for her, but she shook him off and crossed the carpet.

"We'll talk again after breakfast," he said.

"I doubt you'll be up before I leave."

"What?"

At the door, she fixed him with a determined gaze. "This won't continue any longer. I'm going after Fitz, and he will speak to me."

You will not. "You don't know where he is."

"I do, as a matter of fact. Willa has uncovered his location."

A rebuke froze on his tongue and he watched the door close on her.

The stubborn, headstrong woman. He'd no more let her go off on her own to a gentlemen's hunting party then...

Dear God. There'd be little or no rest for him tonight.

At the desk, he reviewed the file of Glanford's unpaid vowels. Sophie had the right of it: it was an ungodly amount. Not impossible, but it would take years and tight purse strings to manage. The loans had begun around the time Father assigned his heir more authority over the Loughton estate.

Fitz had his own small income, but not enough for those loans. Father had handed over the estate management to his eldest, while his second, third, and fourth sons managed investments. Fitz had dipped into the estate funds.

No wonder Fitz was dodging his family. He'd jeopardized Loughton's financial security. Sophie couldn't repay him, so he was struggling to pay others.

George swiped a hand through his hair. He or one of his other brothers should have uncovered this.

He reached for the letters and flipped through them. They were all from Sophie to Fitz, the wax on each unbroken. He put them in date order and began cracking the seals one by one.

As the light sputtered, he collected everything and found his way to his mother's bedchamber.

He wouldn't tell her his plans in a note, even if it meant waking her.

Besides, Mother was never one to hide from the truth. She preferred to know what was going on. She was the strongest woman he knew.

And Sophie was much like her.

***

Unable to sleep, Sophie rose early and was donning her warmest clothes when someone knocked at her bedchamber door. Willa peeked in from the dressing room.

"You're up?" the maid asked. "Who's aknocking at this hour?"

"Shhh. Go back to bed." She crossed to the door.

Lady Loughton's abigail curtsied. "Her ladyship wishes you to join her for breakfast in her private parlor."

"Now?" The delay would set back her plans. She'd hoped to travel to Melton Mowbray and be back by nightfall. She disliked the thought of spending Christmas eve in an inn, away from her boys.

She would do so though, if she must. Now that she'd made up her mind, she wouldn't turn back.

And she'd be able to ask Lady Loughton in person to keep her boys for the duration of her travels instead of leaving a note. "Let me just finish dressing and I'll be right along."

Late the next afternoon...

Once Fitz knew the excuse for George's late morning rousting, he'd shaken off his hangover, had his horse saddled, and begged a fresh horse for George.

Fitz would be madder than Hades when he discovered the lie, but so be it. Mother would deal with him.

A vigilant groom met them in the drive, and the butler opened the door before their boots touched the first step.

"How is Lady Loughton," Fitz asked. "Has the doctor been called?"

Biggs blinked.

"Never mind, Biggs." George tossed his hat and greatcoat, and nudged Fitz toward the stairs. "Seeing her first-born might just be the tonic she needs, despite your two days-worth of beard."

At the door to Mother's bedchamber, Fitz turned on him. "How can you make light of this?"

George reached around him, knocked, and turned the latch.

Mother sat at a table near the fire, a little girl on her lap.

"Papa." Mary jumped off and ran to Fitz.

He swept her up into his arms, his gaze fixed on the older lady. "You are well, Mother?"

"I am now. Or I will be soon."

"Grandmama and I napped together, and now we are reading a book."

Fitz frowned and turned a puzzled look on George.

"You must thank George for bringing you home in time for Christmas," Mother said. "I dare say he's had a very long day of hard riding. Mary, Uncle George will take you back to the nursery, and your papa will pay you a visit after he has had his dinner." She pulled over the stack of letters George had given her in the wee hours. "Fitz, you will come and sit down with me."

"Let me go and change—"

"No. Sit down now, my son. George, have the kitchen send up coffee and a tray." She called the little girl over for a hug.

Fitz watched them, balking.

"Damn it," George whispered. "I'll haul you over and tie you to the chair myself."

His brother pinned him with a glare. "You'll pay for this."

"I've had a look at your books. I fear we'll all pay, and we might as well start facing up to it."

Mary gave him her hand and chattered to him all the way up the stairs.

***

"He's returned," Willa said, entering Sophie's bedchamber with the freshly pressed crimson gown.

"He who?"

"Well, the both of them, Mr. Lovelace and Lord Loughton. Did you rest at all, Sophie?"

After her interview with Lady Loughton, she'd spent the day outside with the children, where their equally matched teams of males and females had battled with snowballs, then returned to her bedchamber with the hope of a nap. "No. I finished the embroidery on the handkerchiefs."

Willa clucked her tongue. "I would've done it while you're having your dinner. I've already eaten with the cook. Had a bit of gossip as well. His lordship was in with her ladyship for a godawful time. Two pots of coffee. Raised voices, they say. Hers or his, they didn't say." She picked up the stays and smoothed a hand over them. "Only reason he came home was he thought she'd taken ill. Shall we start with the dressing now? I've something new in mind for your hair."

Taken ill?

George had lied to his brother, tempting fate with a claim of illness...or...Lady Loughton had allowed him to offer the lie. Oh, how horrid for her, knowing Fitz wouldn't return at a mere motherly request.

"All right," she said. "Have at it. But nothing too complicated I hope."

"You've plans to corner his lordship, I'll warrant. Let's give you something to catch his eye."

"I'm not trying to catch—oh never mind." She surrendered and handed over her hair brush.

All of the children joined them at table for the boisterous Christmas Eve Dinner, even Fitz's daughter, Mary, seated at her Papa's left hand, next to Charlotte, and across from Mr. Cartwright at Lord Loughton's right.

Thankful to be seated further down, Sophie had been placed next to George, the two of them flanked by her boys. Despite the day's travel, George had turned out impeccably groomed and attired. Her hand itched to touch his freshly shaved jaw.

Across the table, Edward picked a bit of dough from his bread, rubbing it into a ball, a sly smile growing until he glanced George's way and popped the morsel into his mouth.

"A formal dinner with so many children," Sophie murmured. "Your mother is very brave."

"You have no idea," he said.

Actually, she had a very clear idea of Lady Loughton's strength of character.

"Thank you for bringing him back," she said.

She'd hoped to speak to George before dinner, but he'd arrived just in time to escort her in.

"I thought it best I make the journey instead of you. You said you're not much of a rider." His gaze swept over her in a trail of heat ending at her bosom. "You look stunning in red."

"Your mother has been loaning me these magnificent gowns." She picked up her wineglass and choked on a sip, suspicion kindling.

Could Lady Loughton be matchmaking? And if so, who did she mean as a match for Sophie?

"But you're wearing a ribbon again. Where is the garnet cross you were wearing the night I arrived?"

Heat raced into her cheeks. The whereabouts of the cross was none of his business. As for the ribbon...

She touched a hand to her neck. "This serves better to cover...a bruise here."

George had the cheek to smile, the bounder.

She hadn't come to Loughton Manor for matchmaking, or to celebrate the Yuletide, nor even to seek a position as a chaperone. She'd come to confront Fitz.

"He's avoiding my eye, I believe," she murmured again.

"No doubt. We'll corner him after he lights the Yule log."

She blinked back sudden moisture. He still proposed to help her.

Under the table, he squeezed her hand and held on, sending her heart soaring.

"If need be, we'll bring Mother into it. And then you and I must speak. There's something I would discuss with you."

"What?"

His smile drained all the joy from her, and she shook her head. "No. I cannot."

One dark eyebrow shot up. "Would you be like Fitz and not even hear me out?" Dropping her hand, he turned to respond to a comment from Artie.

How was she to sit through a boisterous meal, the parlor festivities, the discussion with Fitz and then an indecent proposal?

George's elbow brushed hers and he winked.

"Fustian," she hissed, reminding herself that he was merely a distraction from her true mission.

He squeezed her hand again. "Arthur, tell me about your lands and holdings."

With one ear tuned to Arthur's answer—she'd made sure the new Earl of Glanford knew his responsibilities—she helped Ben manage his peas and his pudding and watched the slow advance of the ormolu clock's minute hand.

***

"You broke into my locked drawer?"

George held Fitz's glare with one of his own. "Needs must, Lord Loughton. What did you expect would happen?"

Fitz walked to the sideboard. "Nothing but sherry?" he growled. "What the devil have you been doing whilst I was away?"

"I might ask the same of you, except I've already discovered the answer. You've been dodging your duties. You've been neglecting mother and the children, including your wards. Sit down, Fitz."

"You impertinent...I ought to flatten you, George."

"And I'd love the chance to knock sense into you. Later. After Sophie has had a piece of you."

Fitz sneered. "Sophie, is it?"

The ass.

"It appears she'll be in perpetual debt to you. I saw the documents. How could you loan so much money to Glanford? Father told you expressly—"

"It was my fault." Fitz filled a glass. "The Matilda Rose." He drained his drink in one long gulp. "Yes, George. I received your warning to get out, after I'd told Glanford all about the golden investment recommended by my wizardly younger brother. I pulled out in time, but I forgot..." He plopped down in the desk chair and rubbed his temples. "I forgot about telling Glanford. Well, and I didn't actually know he'd invested at all, much less put all of his money in. The bloody fool."

The night he'd arrived, Sophie had brought up the Matilda Rose. One loses in one fell swoop.

He'd recommended the investment to Fitz, and Fitz had passed on the tip to Glanford.

"I see." Perhaps Fitz wasn't the only Lovelace Sophie blamed for her troubles.

"The bloody, bloody fool. Always a gambler. When all of his money was gone, including the money Sophie brought to the marriage, he ran through her dower and Ben's trust."

"You should have talked to Father."

"I couldn't."

"Rupert then. Or Selwyn. Or me."

"So you would tell father his eldest is an idiot? Rupert and Selwyn were in London, and you were there as well when you weren't running about the country looking for ore."

Only Mother had known something was wrong, but she'd attributed it to Fitz's personal woes.

Fitz heaved a heavy sigh. "The best solution for Sophie is to marry a wealthy man."

That was the logical solution. The one he would have recommended...before. "Any wealthy man with a head on his shoulder will look into her circumstances."

He certainly would have. Before.

"Not if he's wealthy and head over ears in love. Cartwright couldn't take his eyes off her."

Sophie would marry Cartwright over George's dead body.

"Why don't you marry Miss Parker? Your fiancée will bring a sizeable dowry. You can forgive your ward's debts and carry on. Why not just proceed to the altar with her?"

"Her grandfather is shrewd, and the contracts haven't been signed." Fitz's fingers drummed the desktop. "I suppose the railway scheme will turn a profit one day. How is it progressing? Cartwright was bending my ear about it."

"We've hit a stumbling block." His talk with Arthur at dinner had been informative. He still had a problem to solve there. The boy had proudly described all the Glanford holdings, and the land in question wasn't one of them. "I'll need to leave for Lancashire after Boxing Day and see to an issue."

"Always on the go."

"I'll also need your support in Lords."

"Do tell."

The door creaked, drawing their attention and Mother stepped in, clutching a bundle of letters. Sophie entered behind her.

CHAPTER ELEVEN

"George," Mother said, "bring a chair for Sophie, and all of you be seated please. I must return to Mr. Cartwright. He's been whispering in my ear all day about matrimonial schemes."

Sophie's gaze—normally so cool under duress—met his, and she appeared troubled.

Had Cartwright pressed his suit on her already?

"Nor do I want Mr. Cartwright to interrupt your discussions tonight. Fitz," Mother dropped the letters onto the desk, "I've read all of Sophie's correspondence to you. I suggest you do the same. And here are the others regarding your ward's estate business."

George reached for the second batch. "May I see those?"

She glanced at Sophie, who nodded her permission.

Mother beamed a smile all around. "Fitz will address your concerns, Sophie, and I trust George will offer wise counsel. We shall have a very merry Christmas tomorrow. I will see you in the morning."

As the door closed on her, George sifted through the letters. The steward had written, and tradesmen. But two were postmarked from London, and he recognized the name of the sender. Hands shaking, he unfolded the most recent of the two.

"I am sorry, Sophie," Fitz began, as well he should.

"And I am sorry for your loss, Fitz, and all that has gone before. Now I need you to tell me the state of my son's holdings, and your plans for his future."

Half listening, George began reading.

My dear Lord Loughton,

As mentioned in our letter of 15th November our inquiries have proceeded apace and have uncovered an informal transfer of title for the property in question. As we have been receiving inquiries from a group of investors wishing to secure a right of way for this land, we beg your hasty response so we may properly settle this matter. Be so good as to advise how you would like us to respond to the inquiries we are receiving.

While he read on, Sophie and Fitz spoke of the IOUs, of other debts, of assets, and income, and plans to send Arthur to school.

The words barely registered.

His heart pounded, excitement growing. The land in question, the owner he was supposed to unearth, the person who could approve the right of way, was under the same roof at Loughton Manor.

Or rather...the persons: Arthur owned the land, and Fitz managed it.

And Sophie...

He looked up. Color had risen in her cheeks and her mouth had hardened into a thin line.

What had Fitz said?

Whatever it was, he deserved her anger, and so did Glanford. Her husband had used her, as had Fitz, leaving her struggling to care for the boys while he swanned about with his juggle-headed friends.

Sophie was clear-minded, and honorable, and brave, and she deserved a man who loved her, a business-minded man who would appreciate her intelligence.

Him. He wanted her by his side, forever.

His stomach churned. When she knew about this property, she'd think he was using her as well.

Fitz swiped a hand through his hair. "Very well. You are right. I've bungled everything. I shall empower George to manage Artie's affairs and his education."

"No." George jumped up.

Sophie's eyes widened and her color drained.

He turned away, unable to speak.

If he were empowered, if he used that power to impose the lease...he would be using her. She needed to make the choice.

He cleared his throat and sat down again. "Sophie must have authority to manage Arthur's affairs. She's...clear-minded, honorable, wise. Hand me paper and pen."

***

Head spinning, Sophie stood and began to pace. Shocked and elated, she was also...disappointed. George was fobbing off the responsibility for Arthur. George wanted nothing to do with her.

Oh, what had she expected?

Mr. Cartwright's matrimony scheme must involve George and Charlotte. Perhaps it was the price of his investment in the railway, and George was too honorable to continue leading Sophie on. She wouldn't need to see him again.

That would be fine. That would be better. The kissing, the temptation to touch him, had all been a temporary madness. An unnecessary distraction. She could do this. She didn't need a partner, and it was madness to think a husband would ever be a true partner. And, good heavens, where had that thought come from? Her destination with George had never been the altar.

She took in a breath. Nor would a lover ever be a true partner.

"We'll draw something up right now for the bank, the solicitor and the steward," George said.

His matter-of-fact practicality helped restore her good sense. "I doubt the steward will accept it," she said.

"Then Fitz will extend himself enough to sack him."

"Agreed," Fitz said. "You're traveling that way, George. You'll deliver my letter in person and enforce it. I'll write informing the bank and your solicitor."

The bank and solicitor would speak to her? It was almost too much to hope. "Will this assignment of power be legal?"

George's mouth firmed. "We'll make it so."

Her eyes misted and she turned away. George had seen the extent of her debt. He wanted her out of his hands. He was a sensible businessman, and she and her sons were a financial liability to the entire Lovelace family. George's trip to bring Fitz home had more to do with family honor then any feelings for her. He wouldn't entangle himself with a woman like her.

That would be fine. It must be. Artie's and Ben's futures were all that mattered. The debt was enormous, but she'd negotiate payments. Some of the letters mentioned a proposed property lease. Perhaps it would bring enough for new farm equipment.

And...she had the diamonds. There was no need to spend a season in London with Charlotte now, yet to London she must go.

"I should like to see Glanford's London solicitor, as soon as possible. May I borrow your chaise and leave the boys in your care while I'm gone?"

George's pen ceased scratching and he looked up unsmiling. "I'll accompany you. We'll leave after Boxing Day. I have business there as well."

His transformation almost undid her. Unable to speak, she nodded.

He'd offered to help her, and he had, but not as a friend. Not as a man who cared for her. He'd simply had Fitz dump all of the responsibility on her, and then he would go off and see to his own concerns.

Isn't that what you wanted?

Feeling jumbled inside, she found her voice, wished them a good night, and left.

***

"Oh, for a brandy," Fitz grumbled.

George set down the pen and rubbed his jaw. "In the drawer of the cabinet. Pour me one, as well."

Fitz scoffed. "You hid the bottle?"

"Mother saw to it." He'd left Sophie's letters with his mother while he'd snatched an hour of sleep the night before. When he'd departed before dawn, she'd been awake and quietly furious.

Fitz filled two glasses. "Can Sophie handle the task?"

"A thousand times better than her late husband." Or you.

"You surprise me, brother. I thought turning over Artie to you might help your pursuit. You are pursuing Sophie, aren't you?"

The arrogant fool. He fixed his brother with a glare.

Fitz gasped, and then laughed. "Never say you are seeking more than an affair?"

"Shut up, Fitz."

He tossed back his drink. He would court Sophie when the time was right. She wasn't interested in marriage, she said, but he'd find a way to convince her.

First things first. He needed to be honest with her. He needed to convince her to let his railway run through Artie's land.

"Cartwright," Fitz said. "You're up late."

The blasted man had entered again without George even noticing.

"May I join you?"

"Help yourself to a brandy," Fitz said. "Bring the bottle over."

"Late night business, eh?" Cartwright poured drinks all around. "I saw Lady Glanford departing."

"Yes," Fitz said.

"Your mother told me young Glanford and his brother are your wards, Loughton. Must be difficult, under the, er, circumstances. Troubled estate and all."

George's quill broke, and he reached for a penknife.

"It's always difficult when boys lose their father," Fitz said evenly.

George eased out a breath, and glanced at Fitz. It was difficult to lose a father at any age, especially after losing a wife and child. The Glanford trusteeship had been one burden too many for Fitz.

Cartwright sipped his drink, blissfully silenced.

Perhaps he wouldn't need to use the penknife on the man. He dipped his fresh point in the inkwell.

"Yes, well," Cartwright began again. "Perhaps I can help in that way. And you being the boys' guardian I thought I might as well let you know. I've made up my mind. I intend to offer for Lady Glanford."

George dropped the pen, splattering ink. "Lady Glanford is already spoken for."

Cartwright eyed him shrewdly. "I intend to offer marriage."

Heat fired in him and sent him to his feet, curling his hands into iron fists. Cartwright's implication was clear: he thought George meant to set her up as his mistress.

"If you were a younger man, Cartwright—"

"George." Fitz's sharp reprimand stopped his next words: I'd challenge you. "It's Christmas Eve, George. Mr. Cartwright isn't insinuating anything untoward. He's simply stating his intentions."

"Quite right," the oaf said. "My intentions are honest and honorable. When your mother suggested her for Charlotte's come-out, I had a man look into things. I've a notion Lady Glanford has a grasp of my sort of business as well as estate management, but she won't need to fret about any of it. I can give her a comfortable life. I'm building a new manor in Yorkshire, and have my agent looking for a London home. She can put Glanford behind her. Boys'll be at school. You'll oversee her son's estate, and I'll lift any other worries from her shoulders."

Bile rose in him. Was that what Sophie wanted? She'd gone pale as death at the notion of handling Artie's estate. He needed to ask her.

He slid the paper toward Fitz. "If you would please, finish it before you turn in."

He pounded up the stairs and made his way first to his bedchamber, and then to hers.

***

After a quick stop at the nursery, Sophie found her way to her bedchamber. The room was toasty, the fire burning brightly.

Willa rubbed her eyes and stood. "What time is it?"

"Late. Thank you for waiting up. And good heavens, it's hot in here."

"Cozy, aye. Turn around then. Did all go well?"

"Yes." And no. Her heart twisted. George was back to being the stuffy aristocrat. "Lord Loughton is granting me power of attorney over Arthur and the estate."

Willa froze, and then laughed. "I want to be there when Burford hears that. He won't like taking direction from a woman."

George would be with her when that news was delivered. He hadn't totally abandoned her. "And Burford won't have to. We are sacking him."

Willa whooped. "Praise the Almighty."

She stepped out of the crimson gown and draped it over the chair. While Willa unlaced her stays, she yanked out hairpins.

"Stop wiggling," Willa said. "I never did like the way Burford treated you. He did like your dowry though."

"And sadly, my dowry is gone." Sophie lifted the loosened stays over her head and studied them. "Except for the diamonds, of course. It's time to take them out of hiding. I'm traveling to London this week." And George would be with her for that journey as well.

"I wish you could wear them." Willa carried the dress away. "Your da would have liked that."

Memories rushed her, and she blinked away a surge of shame. She'd been less than gracious accepting the diamonds, astonished at their abundance and size, imagining the whispers about their vulgarity.

Papa had presented them privately, a gift to celebrate the news she'd conceived Glanford's heir. Perhaps an unspoken atonement for what she'd had to endure since her nuptials.

They're just for you, my Sophie. Put them away for a rainy day. Glanford had never known of them, else they'd have been lost in a wager, or draped on the bosom of one of his other women.

She dropped the stays on the bed and retrieved her hairbrush. Willa held out her heavy winter nightgown.

"I'm warm enough in my chemise, and I'm sure your dressing room will be warm now. Go on to bed, Willa."

The maid moved behind her. "Let me just get these pins. There." The last locks of hair brushed her shoulders.

They heard a tapping, and then the latch moved, and George Lovelace stepped into the room.

A fluttering started in the pit of her stomach and spread, sending tingles to the tips of her fingers and toes.

Unsmiling, he hesitated in the doorway, his gaze hooded, his mouth hard.

He turned and closed the door, and she let out a breath.

"Mr. Lovelace," she said.

"Lady Glanford." He stepped closer, and closer still, and swept a hot glance over her body. "Sophie."

Her heart pounded fiercely, hope soaring in her. If he meant to begin a liaison...

What would she do?

She heard the rustle of Willa's skirts.

"Stay, Willa." He drew a small box from under his coat.

He was giving her jewelry?

"Sophie, I wanted to give you my Christmas gift tonight, privately." He reached for her hand and pressed the box in it. "Open it. Please."

"I have nothing for you."

His blue eyes darkened to midnight, sending a shiver through her. Never, never, never had any man unsettled her so.

She summoned her composure. "Very well." The lid snapped open and Willa crowded in.

"Oh," Willa gasped.

Moisture thickened her throat. Her grandmother's cross lay in a bed of white satin between two garnet studded earbobs.

"You b-bought it back." Willa sniffed.

"Yes," he said, his expression still unreadable.

Willa sniffed again and wiped her eyes. "The shopkeeper thought I pinched it. Mr. Lovelace came in and vouched for me."

"And the earrings," he said, "they matched so well, I..."

She flipped over the cross and let her fingertips linger on the faded engraving, the hesitation in his voice touching her. The ever-so-confident Mr. George Lovelace was feeling uncertain.

She eased in a breath. "They're beautiful. But as I said, I have nothing for you."

"About that." George took her free hand and dropped to one knee.

Willa gasped again, and the sound of her sniffing faded as she shuffled away, until the snick of the dressing room door silenced her.

"Sophie. Would you give me your hand in marriage?"

Marriage? Yes, her heart cried.

But her mind picked through the events of the last hour. And the last few days. And the last decade, while she accustomed herself to the notion that George Lovelace was offering her—impoverished, low-born, encumbered with children, Sophie Clark—marriage.

Not a romp, not a brief liaison, but a lifetime of...of what? Respect, and...passion, she hoped. And love?

She blinked back tears. He'd gone mad. They both had. And oh, how she wanted him.

She set aside the box, bent closer, and dropped a quick kiss on his lips.

Pulling away, she set her palm to his jaw and swept her thumb over the masculine stubble there. His eyes glittered up at her, sending more heat through her. "I've been longing to touch you here again."

CHAPTER TWELVE

Luminous eyes gazed down at him from a face otherwise shuttered. She was guarding herself again, and she didn't need to. Not with him.

He stood and embraced her, reveling in the soft heat of her skin under the thin cotton. "Then say yes, you'll marry me." He fisted a lock of her fragrant hair and inhaled deeply. "But, first, hear me out. I need to be completely honest with you."

She backed away and his gaze flew to the swell of her breasts and the curve of her hips under the gown. Color swept up her neck and into her cheeks. "Honest about what?"

A drop of sweat ran down his cheek.

She pulled out a tail of his neckcloth and mopped his face. "Willa appreciates your mother's supply of coal. Now, get on with your confession."

"It's not exactly a confession." He captured her busy hands. "I learned something. Something that impacts you. And Arthur."

Those beautiful eyes widened, searching his face.

"It's potentially very good."

She nodded. "Go on."

"It has to do with right of way leases. One property we wish the line to cross has presented particular difficulties. The title changed hands irregularly. Perhaps as a lost wager? The old owner fled to the continent because of some scandal, and it's taken a great effort to record the transfer. In short, the new owner is the Earl of Glanford."

She let out a long breath. "That's what those letters meant. And you learned this when?"

"Tonight. When I read the solicitor's letter. The one you carried away last night before I could see it. But yesterday, I received a letter that made me wonder. My colleague discovered that the new owner was a minor whose mother was unwilling to allow the right of way." He dropped her hands and mopped his forehead again.

"Take this off."

Her slim hands tugged at his coat, bringing instant relief from the heat of the room, but not from the growing fire inside him.

She patted the back of an armchair. "Sit. Tell me more while I fetch you a drink."

He remained standing, watching her glide into the shadow, wondering how his wooing had transformed into a discussion of business, and whether she minded. Liquid sloshed and she returned with a full glass.

"Only water, I'm afraid."

He thanked her and took a head-clearing drink.

"Better?"

Better would be casting business aside and getting her into bed.

"Yes," he said.

"Tell me more."

"I can understand your objections, Sophie. Use of the land is not without inconvenience to the landowners. The Stockton and Darlington line had to be rerouted to avoid Darlington's fox coverts. Assuming Artie doesn't have fox coverts, there's still the loss of farmland, resistance from tenants, concerns about the smoke and noise—we anticipate using steam engines—and the presence of workmen who are strangers."

"You think I've objected?" There was an edge of irritation in her voice. "Did you not read my letters to Fitz?"

Her letters. Of course. "You didn't know about it."

She bit her lip and perched temptingly on the edge of the wide bed. "Are there tenants? If so, we shall have to hear their concerns."

Hope grew in him, but he'd planned to be brutally honest, so he went on. "And as you so sagely pointed out two nights ago, there may be cost overruns and unexpected pitfalls."

She smiled. "And there's no guarantee the railway won't fail, leaving behind ill will, a disrupted economy and miles of decaying tracks."

Her smile cheered him and he unwound his neckcloth, tossing it aside and seating himself on the bed next to her. "My partners and I have made a solid business plan. We will undoubtedly encounter difficulties, but we will succeed. I won't let you down. I won't leave you penniless. There will be no Matilda Roses in our future. We both have dreams: my railway, your foundry on Glanford land. We can help each other achieve those dreams. We can be true partners. I believe we—you and I—can make a good marriage."

"And a good railway?" She reached for the top button of his waistcoat. "I'm not a natural pessimist, George. The railway will bring more work, more goods for purchase, and faster, safer transportation."

She was, without a doubt, the woman for him. "All of that." And what of my proposal?

"After London," she said, pushing his waistcoat off, "you and I shall travel to Lancashire, see this land, and speak to the people there."

When she smoothed her hand over his clammy shirt, his privy counsellor stirred mightily.

"George, I must ask: did you tell Fitz to give me power over Artie's affairs because you planned to offer marriage and get control anyway?"

"No. Yes—that is, I had—have—no idea whether you will say yes." He closed his eyes and exhaled. "No. I've said I'll be completely honest. I'd planned to wait to ask for your hand. To give you time to take charge of your responsibilities— and they will be your responsibilities, though I'll do everything in my power to help you. I'd hoped to have time to convince you of my love, and that our marriage would be different to your marriage with Glanford. Money will perhaps be tight while you rebuild the estate and I build the railway, but we can make our own fortune, together, as well as see to Artie's and Ben's futures." He touched the warm, silky skin of her bare arms, drinking her in. "I'd planned to wait, but I learned tonight someone else intended to offer for you."

"There are only Fitz and...oh heavens."

Sophie howled and clapped a hand over her mouth, and his heart lifted.

"Cartwright is far richer than I am. I can't offer you a house in town and a country estate—"

"We have a country estate, at least until Artie marries, and then I'll persuade him to give us use of the dower house."

Yes. She was saying yes.

Before he could kiss her, her palm flattened against his chest. "Since we are being completely honest..." She reached for a garment he hadn't noticed and handed it to him.

"Stays."

A husky laugh rippled out of her. "The look on your face, George—let me get scissors."

He fingered the lumpy boning and yellowing fabric, still warm with her heat and her scent, and followed her to the table.

"Feel this." She dragged his finger along the nubby ridge of boning.

"You must order new ones in town. Surely these are paining you."

"It's a reassuring discomfort." She snipped a hole and reached into the casing, drawing out an inch of gold chain.

Gold chain...lumps...Sophie had hidden her jewels.

"I'm not entirely penniless. I know a jeweler in the East End, an old friend of my father's. I shall visit him first thing in London."

She moved the candle closer. Light twinkled and shimmered on one stone, and another, and then another, and a whole string of diamonds until George lost count. "These were my father's gift on the news that I was increasing, that I had fulfilled the Clark commitment to the marriage contract. I hid them from Glanford, and later from creditors, and from the steward. Only Willa knows of them. I would keep them a secret from Fitz, as well."

"Whatever you wish. They are yours."

"There are two more strands like this one. I separated the chains when I hid them. They might bring enough to pay off the loans Fitz is holding."

He squeezed her hand. She'd spared these for so long, he couldn't ask her to part with them now. "We'll work out a payment scheme with Fitz. I'd much rather see you wearing these."

"That might raise a few questions from him," she teased. "As well as from a host of others who settled Glanford's debts for less than they were owed."

"Would you wear them for me in private then?" He picked up the strand and held it to her neck watching her breasts move up and down with sudden emotion, teasing the soft skin with his thumbs. "May we move onto another matter of business?"

"That being?"

"Will you agree to marry by Special License?"

"I..." She swallowed.

"In London?"

"London?"

"This week?"

"George, I—"

Setting the jewels aside, he drew her in for a kiss, one hand holding her, the other loosening the drawstring on her chemise and finally, finally cupping her bare breast.

He would wait, he could wait. If he must. But if he could convince her that sooner was better...

***

The heat of the room was nothing to the fire unleashed within her.

And yet...

Her chemise eased down, and George bent to suckle her, his hand traveling to her rucked-up hem, muddling her mind.

Marry? Next week? In London?

Her first vows had come posthaste, by common license in a church full of strangers, a mere ten days after her compromise. The repenting had gone on for ten years.

She pushed him away and stood, gathering her bodice and covering herself.

George popped up, disheveled, stunned, and...fully aroused. Not angry though. Desire swept through her, and sudden tears swarmed.

He wanted honesty, didn't he? So did she. One more issue must be addressed.

"I was..." She cleared her throat. "A disappointing lover. As you know. Nor did I learn to enjoy..." She squeezed her eyes shut. Bed sport, Fitz had called it.

A calloused finger tucked a lock of hair behind her ear, and stroked down over her neck, the touch gentle.

"What you said that day, George...I know it was perhaps a lack on my part too."

Strong arms came around her then, pressing her face to the soft linen shirt and the hard muscles under it, filling her senses with the spice of his cologne and his own musky male scent. His large hand stroked her back, the touch soothing, reassuring...arousing.

When he set her back from him, he was wearing his businessman's face. "Glanford is dead. You're alive. And I guarantee, you are not disappointing me. What you don't know, I will very much enjoy teaching you. It won't be a chore for me, Sophie, and it won't be for you, if you want me. That is the question, is it not? Do you want me? Am I wrong in thinking that you do?"

The deep midnight blue of his eyes promised everything. But could she be sure?

For years, she'd shoved down her anger and...her disappointment. She loved her boys but she'd never enjoyed the breeding of them. Might it be different with George?

A gasp escaped her. It was already different. "You aren't wrong."

"Then I will begin as I mean to go on—with a well-educated and well-satisfied wife."

She set her palm to his chest, the hard muscle making her shiver.

But they must discuss everything. "I'm older than you."

His smile was wicked. "I know. It doesn't matter. Let me prove it to you."

Finding the air to speak was impossible.

"We won't anticipate our vows." His grin widened. "Not entirely." And then he kissed her and without breaking the kiss, pushed the chemise down and let it fall to her waist, stepping back.

"Like Botticelli's Venus." Laughing, he picked her up and settled her onto the bed. In moments he was shirtless and shoeless and stretched on the bed next to her, all wide shoulders and lean-muscled chest, with a sprinkling of dark hair leading down to—

"What are you grinning about, my lady?" The tip of one calloused finger swept down from her neck, between her breasts, over her belly, down, down until pleasure jolted her.

When his hand moved, her mind turned to mush.

She smiled, and then laughed as he suckled her breast. Pleasure sparked through her, melted her inside, built in her as it had never before done. She'd heard whispers about the pleasure of coupling. Late to the effort, Glanford had tried, making sure she knew it was always an effort he didn't enjoy. Her greatest pleasure had always been him leaving her bed.

"How does that feel, my love?"

George was watching her, his hot gaze making her blood leap.

His love. Her love. Love made the difference.

"Don't stop."

He grinned and resumed his ministrations, and moments later her world exploded.

She came back to earth in his arms and found him eying her, a smug smile softening his features.

"You're still dressed."

"Half-dressed."

"And unsatisfied."

"I am in heaven." His finger lazily circled her breast, sending another jolt of pleasure through her. "Your pleasure, my lady, brings me pleasure."

"I fear...oh." He'd touched a particularly sensitive spot. "Oh, George. I fear you were wrong all those years ago."

"What idiotic thing did I say?"

"You said, 'It takes a woman more than a minute to liven up'." She rolled onto her side and set her hand atop his. "But you were wrong. It only takes the right man."

"And am I the right man?"

"Yes." She laughed. "Most certainly."

***

Early Christmas morning, George slipped on his shoes and shirt and carried his coats back to his bedchamber. Quickly washing, shaving and changing into fresh clothing, he made his way to the nursery, which was already abuzz. The maids were busy wrangling the two youngest into their clothes, while the three half-dressed older boys stretched on the playroom floor engaged in the Battle of Waterloo.

"Not dressed yet?" George said. "You'll want breakfast before church."

Arthur clambered to his feet. James groaned, rising also.

"Church," Edward grumbled.

"No church, no gifts. Now go on, Lovelaces, and finish dressing. Arthur, stay a moment. I would speak with you."

He closed the connecting door to the bedchamber and drew Arthur to the far corner of the playroom, directing him to a stool, and crouching before him.

"I have something to discuss with you—to ask you, really, and I don't want those nodcocks interfering."

Arthur's eyes widened, and he nodded.

"Arthur, I've grown to love and respect your mother. I've asked her to marry me. She has said yes. And I know she'll talk to you, but I wanted to speak to you first. If my mother were to remarry, I'd want to have a say in it. Now, I want to know any objections you might have."

Arthur's eyes pinched together in a frown much like his mother's. "You would be my stepfather."

"That is the way of it. And my brothers, even the two nodcocks you're rooming with, would be your uncles; my sisters, your aunts; my mother, your grandmother."

He worried his lip chewing over those facts.

"You will all be marrying into a great noisy family. I'll treat your mama well, I promise you. You and Ben, also."

"May I go to school with James and Edward?"

George smiled. "Yes. With your mother's approval, which I will do all in my power to obtain. Do I have your blessing?"

Arthur's answering grin displayed a mouthful of healthy white teeth. George shook his hand. "Now, go and get dressed. Your new grandmother expects everyone down for breakfast."

"What's going on here?" Sophie asked from the doorway.

"Mama." Arthur flung himself into her arms. "Merry Christmas, Mama."

She hugged him and glanced over, her eyes glistening. "Mr. Lovelace has spoken to you?"

He nodded.

"And?"

Arthur's grin had frozen in place.

Like his own, he realized.

"You have my blessing, Mama. But may I please go to school with James and Edward?"

"We will talk."

"Mr. Lovelace said he will do all in his power to get your approval."

She tousled his hair and smiled fondly. "Then we shall certainly find a way. Mr. Lovelace can be quite convincing. Now go and finish dressing and I will see you downstairs."

George escorted her out and down the stairs, pausing at the landing and pointing up.

"Oh you." She smiled and rose up on her toes for a kiss that went on, and on, and on.

EPILOGUE

5 January, 1823

"Mama."

Ben burst through the door of Sophie's bedchamber.

His brother snagged his coattail. "You're supposed to knock," Artie said.

"Don't rumple your mama's fine dress," Willa called.

Sophie bent to receive her boys. Attired in coats loaned from the nursery wardrobe, they both looked very fine. "My, but you both are so handsome today."

"So are you, Mama," Artie said.

She ruffled his hair and glanced in the cheval mirror, holding the vision she saw there in her heart. The three of them together—she wished she could capture this in a portrait. Her boys looked well, and so did she. The gown, cream muslin with lace points and scalloped trim, shimmered in the soft morning light. Willa had dressed her hair into intricate coils held with Lady Loughton's pearl-studded combs and laced with blue ribbon.

Something borrowed, and something blue.

But it wasn't just a matter of their attire—the boys glowed with happiness, and so did she.

Lady Loughton appeared in the open doorway. "Are you ready, my dear? I see that your escorts are here, and the carriage has dropped the last passengers and returned. Everyone is at the church except us."

She straightened and took in a steadying breath. Since George's Christmas Eve proposal, her life had been a whirlwind of introductions, and meetings, and even shopping.

The gown was new, made especially for her with her own money.

Something new.

And then there'd been the rushed travel, long days in the cold of this bitter winter, short nights in inns, so that they might reach Loughton Manor by Twelfth Night.

"Come along, dear ones. We'll wait for your mother downstairs." Lady Loughton ushered the boys to the door and sent Sophie a wink. "Don't delay. George is not known for his patience."

Her boys would forever draw a full share of Lady Loughton's kindness. It was enough to make her weep.

Oh, but she mustn't. Not until later.

Willa held up the sky-blue redingote for her to slip into. "There now," she said, tugging her over to the mirror again. "You look more like a countess now than ever you did before."

She squeezed Willa's hand. "And I'll come home a mere missus."

"Ye'll always be a lady, my girl." Willa's eyes brimmed, and she turned away.

Sophie squeezed her own eyes tight, gathering her composure. She would not walk down the aisle with red eyes.

When Willa finally spoke, she was her usual bustling self. "It's time we should go," she said, coming to stand with Sophie, and smiling at the mirror. "Glad you kept the biggest one. Your da would be that pleased."

A single diamond in a setting of gold twinkled at her throat.

Something old and very precious.

With Artie and Ben crowded in the carriage beside her, she put aside her own butterflies, and relished their joy. At the church steps, Artie handed her out with grave dignity. In the vestibule, a Loughton Manor footman took their cloaks, then Willa made one final tweak of the gown and slipped through the sanctuary door behind Lady Loughton.

Every nerve in her body came alive and she paused, searching for her composure again. She had no cause to be nervous, and all the reason in the world to be excited.

George, bless him, had secured a common license so they could marry at his village church, with her boys and his family present.

"What are we waiting for?" Ben grabbed her hand.

Artie frowned up at her, his face filled with concern. "Are you ready, Mother?"

Perhaps he was worried she would change her mind. Her serious little earl had already begun asking George about investigating for ore.

"I am." She kissed both of them, slipped her hand over Artie's arm, and stepped through the sanctuary door.

Eager faces turned toward her, the pews jammed with people, both great and small. The whole village was in attendance.

And at the altar, George looked her way, a smile blooming on his handsome face, warming her all the way to her toes.

She glanced down at her boys' astonished faces, and laughed.

And walked down the aisle to her waiting groom.

Later that evening...

Downstairs, while the Twelfth Night festivities with family, neighbors, and friends continued, George and Sophie slipped away, leaving the boys in the care of their grandmother, and sending Willa back to the party below stairs.

When the door closed on the maid, George shed his coat and pulled Sophie into a kiss, all the while working the fastenings of her gown.

She backed away, laughing, her bodice slipping. "Tired of waiting, are you, Mr. Lovelace?"

He breathed a kiss on her neck that made her shiver. "Are not you, Mrs. Lovelace?" he murmured.

Since Christmas Eve, George hadn't done more than kiss her, though the kissing had been quite thorough.

She clutched his hand and stepped out of her gown and the stays he'd loosened without her noticing. "Tired of you making me wait, yes."

"Impatient, are you?" He waggled his eyebrows, unbuttoning his waistcoat, tossing it aside, and doing the same with his neck cloth and shirt until he was down to his trousers. He propped his hands on his hips and puffed out his handsome chest. "Mayhap that was part of my strategy, Mrs. Lovelace."

Desire simmered along every nerve, squeezed the breath from her lungs, heated and pooled until she was ready to welcome him.

She eased out one comb and then another, and another, watching him, as he watched her.

"Your strategy sir," she said raking her hands through her hair, "is working."

In a flash, he shed the rest of his garments— and made hers disappear also, and then carried her to the bed.

"My dear, Sophie," he murmured, "my dear darling wife."

And then he kissed her, and there was no more need for words.

The End

A Note from the Author

I hope you've enjoyed Sophie and George's story, Book 2 in my Upstart Christmas Brides Series!

George Lovelace first appeared in *The Duke She Despised* part of 2019's *Winter Wishes Regency Holiday Romance Anthology*, a USA Today bestselling collection of holiday romances. *The Duke She Despised* is now available as a stand-alone romance.

A third story in this series will appear next fall in the *Christmas Kisses* anthology, now available for preorder. George's brother, Fitz, will get his happily-ever-after!

Research for this story took me into the exciting period in British history when railways were just a dream of enterprising Brits. As usual, my characters and story are entirely fictional, and any historical errors are mine alone.

Many thanks go to editor Tessa Shapcott, and as ever, I'm grateful to my husband for his unfailing support.

I love hearing from readers! Please follow me on Facebook, Bookbub, Pinterest, and at my website, AlinaKField.com. And for monthly news about releases and sales, sign up for my newsletter at my website. I promise I won't spam you or sell your email address!

Best regards and happy reading!

Alina K. Field

Books by Alina K. Field
Sons of the Spy Lord Series

Marrying Mr. Gibson

Previously titled *The Bastard's Iberian Bride*

Paulette Heardwyn rushes to visit her dying guardian, set on learning the truth about her father. But the only man with answers takes his secrets to the grave, leaving her penniless—unless she marries his illegitimate son

The Viscount's Seduction

Lady Sirena Hollister has lost everything, even her fey abilities. But when the fairies hand her a chance at a London Season, her schemes for revenge stir up an unknown enemy, and spark danger of a different sort, in the person of a handsome Viscount.

The Rogue's Last Scandal

Falling—literally—into the arms of the *ton*'s most outrageous rogue seems a risky path of escape, but Maria Graciela Kingsley y Romero has no other choice. Only England's greatest spy lord can help her, and he is not to be found—so his son will have to do!

The Counterfeit Lady

Vowing she'll never submit to an arranged marriage, an earl's daughter bolts for the seaside cottage that will someday be hers. But she finds her quiet refuge occupied by the last man she ever wants to see—an American artist, who's also a thief. And, quite possibly one of her father's spies.

Avenging the Earl's Lady

The long war is over, but honor requires vanquishing one last enemy, and the Earl of Shaldon has no time for romance. But when the lady he longs for interferes in his plot, and his enemy strikes at her, nothing else matters but avenging his lady.

Novellas and Holiday Stories

The Marquess and the Midwife
A Christmas Novella
Finalist, 2016 National Reader's Choice Award

Uncovering a lie drives a new marquess back from a self-imposed exile at Christmas to find the only woman he's ever loved. Finding her turns out to be easy, uncovering her stunning secrets, a bit harder. But winning her back will be the greatest challenge of all.

A Leap Into Love
A Sweet Regence Romance Novella, a sequel to
The Marquess and the Midwife

Can a gentleman be too charming?
The ladies of Upper Upton think so.
When the single ladies of the village conspire to teach their charmer a lesson that might bankrupt him, the town's loveliest young widow—who's sworn off marriage forever—steps up to warn him.

Liliana's Letter
Finalist, 2015 National Reader's Choice Award

The Matchmaker Meets the Matchbreaker

Liliana Ashford's future as a professional chaperone depends on her wealthy charge's successful marriage, but her own close encounter with a scoundrel years ago makes her determined to save the girl from the same kind of rogue.

The Ghost of Depford Hall
A short, sweet Halloween story, a sequel to
Liliana's Letter

It's her mother's last All Hallows' Eve.
When family, friends, and tenants gather, goblins, ghouls, and ghosts are banned from this All Hallows' Eve party.
Only, no one told the Ghost of Depford Hall!

Courted by the Earl
Previously titled *Bella's Band*
A 2015 RONE Award Finalist
Saddled with his brother's title and debts, nothing about
this new life makes the Earl of Hackwell want to stay—until
he meets a lady with a secret that can change everything.

Rosalyn's Ring
2014 Book Buyer's Best Winner, Novella Category
Done with grieving her losses, a late nobleman's daughter
has fallen into a tidy spinster's life in London. But when one
snowy Christmas Eve, a young woman needs rescue, she
seizes the chance to do good—and to recover a family heirloom that ought to be hers.

Haunting Miss Fenwick

Thrilled to finally have a permanent home, a Squire's
daughter won't let a supernatural creature scare her away.
While hunting the ghost she doesn't believe in, she stumbles
upon a mysterious flesh and blood man who might be the
key to all of her problems.

The Duke She Despised
Book 1 in the Upstart Christmas Brides Series

Hiding her true identity, a young vicar's widow takes a position as housekeeper in a remote Scottish castle at Christmas
for a new duke who years ago sabotaged her chance for happiness. She quickly falls for the duke's charming but not
very competent factor, not knowing that he's hiding something also—he's the duke she despised!

The Macbeth Series

Fated Hearts
A Love After All Retelling of the Scottish Play
A Scottish Baron returning from two decades at war meets
the wife he divorced and the daughter he disavowed before
she was born, only to learn that everything he'd believed
was a lie. Determined to win back the only woman he's ever
loved he must first face the viper who drove them apart.

The Comtesse of Midnight
In the *Storm & Shelter Bluestocking Belles and Friends Anthology*
Coming April 2021

A Scottish Earl on a quest for the elusive Comtesse de Fontenay, rescues a French lady smuggler during a devastating storm, taking shelter with her. As the stormy night drags on, he suspects she knows the lady he's seeking, the lady who holds the secret to his identity. When she admits she herself is the Comtesse de Fontenay, just not the one he's seeking, she dashes all his hopes—and promises him new ones.

Find out more at
https://AlinaKField.com
and sign up for my monthly emails
for news about upcoming books and
sales.